Freedom's Fight:
A Call To Remember

SUSAN J. CALLOWAY KNOWLES

ISBN-10: 0615787029
ISBN-13: 978-0615787022

DEDICATION

This book is dedicated to all those Americans who believe that they were endowed with God given rights and freedoms that will always be worth fighting for even when challenges at times to those rights and freedoms appear insurmountable!

TABLE OF CONTENTS

ACKNOWLEDGMENTS

I would like to acknowledge all those who lovingly encouraged me to write this book because you believed in me.

PROLOGUE

America's values have given way to the Regime's ideologies. The Regime has imposed its philosophy of "benefitting the collective at the expense of the individual" as what is needed in the new Aplitacon society so that everyone can be made "equal."

The Regime will stop at nothing to convince the once-free America that the "gain" to be achieved for the collective far outweighs the loss of individual freedom.

Bethany's memories of family and lessons from childhood will be all that she and those brave enough to fight will have to arm themselves with in order to reclaim the country they once knew before the Regime came into power.

Only those who remember a better way of life and their God given freedoms will have a chance to answer the call of "Freedom's Fight" before freedom is lost forever.

May God bless America!

CHAPTER 1:
LIFE'S LITTLE BLESSINGS

"How long have I been sleeping?"

I could hear these words replaying in my mind as they had so many times before. This time, the words startled me the rest of the way awake. I sat straight up. My heart pounded as I tried to get my bearings of where I was and what time it could possibly be.

I had been sleeping on the hard ground in my red plaid sleeping bag, still zipped halfway up to keep out the cool morning air. It appeared to still be early morning because the ground was damp with the late fall dew. The mountain air was somewhat chilly, which required me to have to zip my green lightweight jacket all the way up to keep out the cool breeze that lingered on my face. The sky was a light blue with just a hint of fog hovering above as the sun continued its rise over the top of the mountainside that surrounded me. The yellow and red fall leaves stirred about on the ground each time the breeze picked up and then subsided. Birds flitted from one branch to another overhead, quietly yet methodically searching for their morning breakfast in preparation for their day.

It was becoming increasingly difficult to live this type of lifestyle. Waking up on the ground every morning had been easier when I was in my teens and even my twenties. Now, however, in my late thirties it was becoming more of a struggle. What would life be like waking up in a sleeping bag in my sixties? Fall and winter were the worst times of the year for me. I could typically find some shelter to protect me from the winds, rain, and cold snowfalls. However, I had to move quickly in order to locate temporary shelter, such as an empty restroom in a park or other makeshift shelter, before others beat me to it. This might be more difficult to accomplish throughout my senior years. I didn't want to think about it now, though.

Also, the weather in the mountains of North Carolina and its changing seasons had already begun to take its toll on my fair skin. It's not something you relish if you are like most females. There had been a time after my awkward teenage years that I had actually become comfortable in my own skin. Now my skin seemed to be growing more uncomfortable with me because of all the harshness I was putting it through by spending most of my days and nights outside and exposed to the elements. There was nothing I could do to change that. Not now, maybe not ever.

My grumbling stomach interrupted my thoughts. My stomach had been relatively empty for a while. It was nothing new. Food was hard to come by. I wondered aloud at how long it had been since I had eaten anything substantial. At the moment, as I was trying to unzip my sleeping bag and stand up, I wasn't really sure. My definition of substantial had changed over time as well. Substantial now meant even a couple of bites of food. Substantial rarely meant a full meal these days.

Thinking about food made me remember the last conversation I had with an old man I met in town two days ago. That was the last time that I had eaten anything of significance. It was his generosity that was significant and what I remembered most about that day rather than the amount of food he offered me.

He had seemed like such a kindhearted man. I first saw him while he was walking with a young girl—who I later learned was his granddaughter—around a fenced-in play area that appeared as though it had fallen in disrepair some years ago. All that remained viable were two small swings that hung side by side from chains secured to the rusting bar above. I watched as this man gently lifted his granddaughter, who appeared to be approximately four years old, up onto the swing's seat, taking his time to ensure that she wouldn't fall and get injured.

I heard her shout, "Push me real high up, grandpa."

5

The man had smiled at her and then moved the swing forward before letting go of the chains that he held in both hands. I watched as the swing was propelled forward and then back as the young girl sat dangling her small legs freely in the air, laughing each time he pushed the swing forward again.

Finally, when the little girl had tired of swinging, her grandfather looked up and noticed that I had been watching them. He waved at me and smiled.

I had been standing in the road near the play area watching them enjoy their time together. I hesitated a moment and then slowly lifted my hand to acknowledge his wave. I must have looked harmless enough to him because he grabbed his granddaughter off of the swing and quickly led her over to where I was standing.

"Hi, my name's Buck," he said. "How are you?"

"I'm fine," I replied without offering my name.

It had been an awkward moment as I tried to look him more directly in his eyes.

He continued, "Would you care for something to eat? I don't have much but we've eaten and we have extras."

I had felt so embarrassed when he asked me this question. I had never gotten over the shame that I felt when I was hungry and had been offered food by someone, usually a stranger. My parents had not raised me to live off of strangers' generosity. However, it had become a way of life.

He noticed my discomfort and offered me a muffin from a bag before I could even answer. I hadn't seen him carrying the bag that must have been sitting on an old picnic table near the swings. I reluctantly took the muffin and thanked him. I could immediately tell that the muffin was homemade because the blueberries were rounder and bigger than in the store-bought muffins. At least, that's how I remember homemade muffins looking.

"I'm sorry, that's all I have to offer you this morning, Miss," he said.

As he smiled, the slight breeze gently tossed what was left of his dark hair.

"Please, no, I'm fine. You are very kind, thank you," I managed to say as he nodded his head, acknowledging my appreciation.

"Yes, ma'am I'm glad to help out."

I had thanked him again for the muffin and left them in the play area before walking back the same way I had come.

A few days ago, I had stumbled upon a small town just off the gravel road on which I had been walking. The weather had been similar to today's weather. The skies had been clear with a brisk wind to remind me that winter was coming soon.

I hadn't run into too many people while walking on the road because most people wouldn't choose to be walking like I was, off the beaten path. Rather most would choose to sit comfortably in their homes.

I didn't choose this life. It was something that was chosen for me years ago. I could feel myself becoming tense with anger when I thought about it. How did I get here? Why had I allowed myself to end up living life this way? These were the thoughts I carried with me most days. My other thoughts focused on survival. Where would I eat? What would I eat? Would someone discover that I was alone and try to hurt me? These were not the thoughts that I had as a child growing up in the mountains of North Carolina. These were my thoughts now, nonetheless, following the election of the Regime.

CHAPTER 2:
LESSONS LEARNED

My living situation had become so difficult over the years that I started relying on my memories to keep me going. My parents always told me as a child how important my memories would become someday. I wasn't sure at the time what they meant but these days I was starting to understand it better.

My mother especially, would have many conversations with us about the importance of family and the memories that are made within each family. One of the conversations that I remember most occurred when I was about eleven years old. We had all gathered around the kitchen table, as most families used to do in those days, to have dinner together. It was always my responsibility to set the table for our meals since I was the oldest. It was a responsibility that I wasn't always thrilled with doing but one that my mother insisted on.

My mother had been bequeathed dishes over time from relatives who had passed away. They were treasures of sorts to her. Although I wasn't happy about setting the table each day, I was always cognizant of the significance of these dishes to my mother. As such, I carefully carried each plate to the table as though they were made of gold.

On this particular summer day, I was in a hurry to eat dinner and return to playing outside with my sisters. I wanted to finish a game that we had started earlier in the day. My mind wandered away from setting the table to wondering where I could find more dirt to create a higher pile for us to ride our bikes through. We had been running our bicycles back and forth through the dirt pile most of the day. I had wanted to make the pile even higher and contemplated putting a wooden ramp against it so that we could jump over it rather than through it. I remember thinking that day that all I wanted to do was stay outside forever. Dinner was temporarily interfering with that daydream.

> *"Be careful, hon," Mom said as I hurried to place the last dinner plate at my father's spot on the kitchen table.*

> *"Don't worry, Mom," I answered back. "I'm not going to break great-granny's dish," I said with a smirk on my face, as any eleven-year-old would who didn't yet understand the value of memories.*

> *"I know you are being careful, sweetie," Mom replied, "but your great-grandmother worked hard to buy those dishes after she and your great-grandfather celebrated their first five years of marriage. She loved them so much and we used to have many great meals on those plates."*

My mother would then generally continue on for a few minutes with stories that had enthralled her while listening to her parents and grandparents talk around the kitchen table during her childhood. My sisters and I would usually roll our eyes at each other during her storytelling, especially when it was about the third time she had recounted a particular story.

Little did I know then that I would one day fondly reminisce about my mother's childhood stories. It was not until my adulthood that I was able to understand and appreciate the fact that the "value" of the dishes had nothing to do with the dishes themselves. Rather, their importance came from the lives of the people who owned them, lives that carried with them meaningful stories that would be passed on from one generation to another—accounts that would offer the listener rich cultural family traditions unique to their own time periods and ideologies.

My parents also encouraged me to remember as much as I could from what I had gained from listening to other people, studying in school, reading books, and living life in general. They told me that a valuable education was one that went beyond books and encompassed the entire learning process throughout a person's life. They stressed that this knowledge would serve to inspire and protect me throughout my life. I wasn't sure of all the things that I needed protection from but as a child I didn't question my parents' wisdom. That didn't prevent me from complaining to my parents, however.

> *"But, I don't want to read history tonight, Daddy! Why do I have to learn this stuff anyway? I don't care who discovered America or what Hitler did," I would proclaim. "So, what, America's been discovered, big deal and Hitler's dead! That stuff is old news."*

> *My father would wait patiently until I finished my childish tantrum. Then slowly and lovingly he would explain the importance of understanding history.*

> *"Understanding history and why things happened the way they did can help you to comprehend the future."*

> *"That's dumb, Daddy," I would retort with a cynical teenage tone.*

> *"Bethany, history has a way of repeating itself," my father calmly explained, "and unless you learn about it you won't know if the same mistakes are being made again without you even realizing it."*

All I knew was that there was television to watch and history was keeping me from it. I had no desire to learn history because in all of my wisdom at the age of thirteen, I knew that I would have no need for it in my life. I was wrong but would not come to realize it until I was much older and recalled what my father had been trying to teach me that day. He was trying to assist me in recognizing that unless you study the enemies of the past, you won't recognize them when they return.

They had returned and the American people had not recognized the enemy in its new disguise. The Regime had a new face but a familiar agenda; an agenda that my parents had been preparing me for during my childhood without me realizing that I would one day come face-to-face with it.

CHAPTER 3:
FOND MEMORIES CAN BRING BOTH JOY AND PAIN

There are times when my memories are all I have to cling to now. They pull me through the hard times. Not all of my memories bring me joy, however. Some memories are bittersweet because the joy of a past event was so joyous that looking back on it now only brings pain. For this reason, there are some memories that quite frankly, I would rather forget.

Some of my first and fondest memories from my childhood are of me playing in wooded mountain areas with my sisters. The trees were huge and daunting to such a young child as me. I can still remember the fallen tree branches snapping underneath my feet as I would wander off well-worn paths. The dirt was rich and the land was for playing in my eyes. I spent hours pretending that I was searching for cowboys and Indians who might be hiding in the woods. I would plan how I could sneak up and capture them before they saw me. I wouldn't know until many years later that this children's game would become my preparation for harder, menacing times as an adult living with the real opponent.

> *"Stop right there, Priscilla," I shouted at my sister from behind the tree. "You are under arrest for stealing the stagecoach and all of its loot belonging to the Mountain Pass Stagecoach Company."*

I pointed the stick that I was using as my gun to capture the "bad guys", toward my sister. Today, my sister, Priscilla was one of the bad guys whom I would be arresting.

Priscilla, who was sitting on an old picnic table in our backyard that we had temporarily dubbed as a stagecoach, sat quietly with both hands held high in the air as a sign of surrender. I had chased her down from the woods on my imaginary horse while she tried to get away in the stolen pretend stagecoach.

"All right," I said. "Throw down that money and jump down here."

Priscilla, being careful not to allow her make-believe horses to begin running at the feel of loosened reins, tied the reins meticulously around the brake with one hand while the other hand remained in the air. A long stick placed next to the chair in which she was sitting atop the stagecoach was being used as a brake holding the stagecoach in place.

Priscilla slowly stood up, hands still reaching high into the air, and descended the stagecoach by using an old wooden box that acted as steps. It was time to disarm her now that she was safely on the ground.

"Move slowly, unbuckle your gun belt, and let it hit the ground," I said in my toughest sheriff's voice.

Priscilla took her left hand and easily unbuckled her belt. My father's belt had substituted for a real gun belt and sticks, used to exemplify her guns, fell swiftly onto the ground when the belt was released.

We would then trade places and another game would ensue in which cowboys would chase Indians and Indians would track cowboys until we were called in from our play.

The memories of my sister and I playing together that summer, while pleasant, sometimes takes its toll on me because of the longing I feel for those happier times. The sadness and yearning I experience hinder me when I'm busy just trying to survive. It's during those times that I need to keep my focus on the present and not allow my mind to return to a period in my childhood when I was free. Free from worry and doubt about what might occur tomorrow, or even today for that matter, all due to the Regime's restrictive policies.

There are many other memories that I find myself dwelling upon to find comfort. On days when I have been able to secure something to eat I can think back to when I was at home enjoying Thanksgiving with my family. That seems so long ago now. However, the aromas are easily remembered on the good days.

> *"Mom, I think Aunt Kimmie and Uncle Kyle are coming," I shouted as I raced through the house to the front door.*

> *"Slow down Bethany. You're going to fall down," my mother shouted back.*

> *I could see my aunt and uncle getting out of the rental car that was parked in our driveway. My Aunt Kimmie was my mother's sister and lived out of state with her husband, Kyle. Usually my aunt and uncle would come to our house each year to celebrate either Thanksgiving or Christmas. My aunt was in her fifties and for as long as I could remember she was elegantly dressed on any occasion. This occasion would be no exception.*

> *My aunt stepped out of the car wearing what appeared to be a tan lightweight wool skirt with a white silk blouse. I couldn't quite make out from the front door what kind of pin she was wearing on her blouse, but my aunt never went anywhere without some kind of pin. Typically, she would wear a garnet brooch that had been given to her by her wealthy boss. My aunt was a personal assistant to a stockbroker on the west coast. We never knew much about him other than that he was rich. My aunt was a walking example of just how rich he was because his wealth was always prominently displayed in the clothing she wore and in the jewelry he gave her. My Uncle Kyle seemed happy to let my aunt's boss buy these gifts for her because it meant that he didn't have to buy them—not that he could have anyway.*

My aunt usually brought something special for our Thanksgiving dinner. Thanksgiving was such a happy time for me. I remember my mother would spend several weeks before Thanksgiving planning the family meal. Our meal would normally center around a huge turkey. One that would feed at least seven or eight people, depending on how many family members were planning to stop by to celebrate with our family of five; my mother, father, my younger sisters, and myself. Typically, my grandmother and grandfather would always be there. At other times, several of our cousins might drop in. It was always an enjoyable time on Thanksgiving

Day. My mother, eager to feed her family a meal that showed her love, would rise early in the morning while we were still sleeping. We could hear her preparing the turkey to go into the oven for its five to six hours of baking. After stuffing the turkey, she would place it securely on a rack in the oven and then hop back into bed for a couple of hours while it baked.

My mother would spend the rest of the day baking the remainder of the meal, which usually consisted of mashed potatoes and gravy, green beans, yams, bread, stuffing, and pumpkin pie. This was the yearly menu unanimously voted on by my family. I'm not sure why we even voted on the menu every Thanksgiving because the menu was always the same. No one ever complained, however. The house on that special day was filled with aromatic roasting turkey, nutmeg and cinnamon from the yams, pumpkin pie filling, and piping hot bread with butter oozing down the sides. Everyone sat around laughing and conversing with each other for hours, catching up on day-to-day things and remembering holidays past.

"Aunt Kimmie, I'm so glad you're here," I cried as I ran to hug her, not wanting to wait until she came inside the house and disappeared with all the adults.

"Bethany, you've grown so much," Aunt Kimmie said. "Come and help us get some things out of the car. I think I have a little something for you and your sisters," she said with a little wink.

"Uncle Kyle, hi," I said, not wanting to ignore him and appear more interested in the gift from Aunt Kimmie than in seeing him.

"Where's your mother, sweetie?" Aunt Kimmie asked.

"She's in the house working on the turkey," I replied.

"Well, let's go in and say hello, then," Aunt Kimmie said with a cheerful smile that brightened her green eyes under her sandy blonde hair.

As we opened the door to go back inside the house, aromas of turkey and a myriad of desserts filled our nostrils.

Thinking about those Thanksgiving days on mornings when I have not eaten well in a while only serves to bring me down.

I knew that I couldn't afford to dwell on the past today because I couldn't allow myself to become emotionally weak. I need to stay strong mentally and physically to survive what may lie ahead. And what lay ahead was anyone's guess.

Suddenly, I realized that I had been thinking back about better days for far too long. I needed to stay focused in order to not be seen by anyone who could be walking around the area. It could prove to be detrimental if I stayed too long in one place. The need to not be found outweighed my hunger for food and my desire to concentrate on happier moments in my life. There would be time for sleep later on tonight and perhaps a chance to dream about pleasant childhood memories, if I was lucky.

CHAPTER 4:
CAPTURED REFLECTIONS - A GRANDFATHER'S LOVE LOST FOREVER

I hurriedly rolled up my sleeping bag and reattached it to the cumbersome black backpack that was on the ground next to me. The backpack was often too heavy for me to carry because I had it weighted down with a number of things that I thought I would need. One of my prize possessions was a silver flashlight that I had been carrying for years. I used it sparingly, however, because batteries were hard to come by. I also had a small black metal frying pan that my mother once used in our home to cook our meals on, as well as several pairs of shoes that I had found while walking around, various shirts, pants, socks, underwear, matches, and some cans of food.

It was also not unusual for me to have a few cans of pork 'n beans stuffed in the corner pocket on either side of my backpack. Any time I reached for a can of beans, I remembered my grandfather joking that a person could never have too many beans. He was always making some joke about something. He was such a happy man. I was never sure why he was so happy. It made me laugh to be around him. Thoughts of my grandfather make me smile even when I'm having a bad day.

He was a kind man. My mother said that he was the best father that she could have ever hoped for when she was growing up. I understand that now because as a child he was the best grandfather that I could have ever hoped for. It was the little things that he did that meant so much to me.

One of my favorite memories that continues to bring me much comfort on days when I'm struggling is the memory of watching my grandfather shave in front of the big mirror on his dresser. In those days, most dressers also came with a huge mirror that spread across the entire length of the dresser. A person could not only stand in front of their dresser to retrieve their clothing from the drawers, but they could also comb their hair, put on their make-up, or shave.

I can still picture this shaving ritual clearly in my head as if it were yesterday. It would begin on most mornings, with my grandfather grabbing a white ceramic mug, placing some facial soap and some warm water into the bottom of it, and then getting a facial brush to lather up the soap. The ceramic mug wasn't a typical lightweight coffee mug either. It was designed specifically to be used for shaving, which meant that it was a thicker, heavier mug that could have been mistaken for a coffee mug except that it weighed more. His facial brush usually consisted of a wooden handle about three inches long with soft tan bristles extending out of the bottom of the handle. Once my grandfather had determined that the lather was thick enough, he would apply the soap to his face.

I would sit quietly holding my breath and eagerly watching how my grandfather went through his graceful routine, memorizing every step he made. It was almost like watching a ballet. Each movement seemed in perfect timing with the next. I studied his shaving routine closely as often as I could. I recall that I would sit on his bed behind him and just watch the swishing of his facial brush down into the cup until just the right moment before he applied the soap to his bearded face. He would then pick up a razor blade holder (typically made out of stainless steel in those days), open it carefully and allow a razor blade to fall securely in place before closing the top over the blade.

Next, he would gently shave his face, being careful not to press too hard so that he wouldn't cut himself with the sharp razor blade. He would usually start at the top of one of his cheeks and make his first swiping motion downward, removing the wet soap as he went. He did this on both cheeks until he was ready to shave underneath his nose. At that point, my grandfather would take his index finger and carefully lift his nose straight up in the air so that he could get a better angle with the razor. I used to remark that it made him look like he was turning his nose up at something he didn't like. He would end his shaving procedure by making long upward strokes to shave off the whiskers on his neck. I could recreate his shaving routine in my sleep. I had seen it a million times and I never tired of it.

I envied his routine because I couldn't be a part of it. Nor would I ever be. I was a girl and girls didn't shave their faces. It saddened me because I wanted to share in this with my grandfather. Even as a young child around nine years old, I knew that shaving together would enhance our relationship. My grandfather, being the kind and wonderful grandfather that he was, must have read my mind.

I can remember one special occasion when I was sitting on my grandfather's bed, preparing for him to start the shaving procedure that I had come to know and love. It was our time together. What surprised me as I sat there was that this day would be different than all the rest.

My grandfather went to the sink to pour warm water in his shaving mug so that he could begin to lather up the soap like he had done so many times before. But he did something else this time that I wasn't expecting. He grabbed another ceramic mug, dropped a bar of soap inside, filled it with a small amount of water, and then grabbed a second facial brush. Afterwards, he turned toward where I was sitting and asked me if I would like to join him. I was beaming as I caught my reflection in the dresser mirror.

"But Grandpa," I asked, "how can I join you if I can't shave my face?"

He just looked at me with the pure love that only a grandfather can have for his granddaughter and replied, "Sweetheart, don't worry. We don't have to put a blade in your razor."

Why hadn't I ever thought of that? At nine years old, I guess some issues of logic escape you. However, my grandfather had put two and two together and had realized that I wanted to bond with him by sharing in this experience. We both stood side by side at the dresser that day, swishing our brushes into our mugs, shaving our faces, and laughing as the lather on our faces made us both look like Santa Claus. It was a day that I would never forget.

But it was a day and a memory that was gone forever for all families. The Regime has made sure of it, since they did not believe in such idleness even within one's own family and would put an end to it by their repeated propaganda campaigns against waste. There would no longer be an ability to share precious moments with loved ones as I had once shared with my grandfather.

Even the familiar ceramic mug would be considered intolerable by the Regime because they would deem it harmful to the environment and in need of banning. The bar of soap used by my grandfather would also be earmarked as wasteful and replaced with a premeasured and prepackaged liquid instead.

The Regime would take their regulations one step further today by requiring a granddaughter to turn her grandfather in for his selfish anti-environmental antics. Life was different under the Regime's rules and there seemed to be no end in sight to what was being enacted on a daily basis by their leadership. It was a frightening proposition to say the least.

CHAPTER 5:
OUT WITH THE OLD

I needed to put the time with my grandfather behind me. Daydreaming about the special time I shared with him was not going to put food in my stomach. I kept reminding myself that today was a day that I would need to clear my head if I hoped to find any food and a warm place to sleep later on. Sleeping in my sleeping bag in the open air was becoming harder to do now that winter would soon be arriving. My sleeping bag had been issued to me when I was sixteen years old. It was still in relatively good shape even though it was now twenty-two years old. We both had been in better shape, I thought to myself. Although I was only thirty-eight years old, I had seen and experienced a lot, which made me feel much older. The Regime had issued everyone sleeping bags. We were supposed to be given sleeping bags every five years but I decided not to take the Regime's hand out.

It seemed that we were always being provided something. Most people considered getting things provided for free as a good thing. I knew better and I knew that I didn't want to be a part of it. I watched throughout my life as everyone got the same amount of whatever it was and all in the same color. No matter what, you never saw anyone else with something different than what you had. Every person received the same red plaid sleeping bag, the same amount of weekly food, the same type of housing unit with the exact same number of rooms. Even the furniture inside the units was the same color, shape, and assortment of items. It was boring to say the least.

The sameness of everything had the effect of sucking the energy right out of you — if you were a thinking person that is.

It had all begun with the governmental Regime. There were some who welcomed the takeover of the Regime. Some had even argued for the Regime and the elimination of America's capitalism. Capitalism had been a way of life in America for more than two centuries, according to my grandparents. It was a way for people to earn what they needed and to fulfill their potential in life. My father always said that in America you could become a millionaire if you were willing to work hard enough. My grandparents had cautioned us early on when we were growing up that the government was always awaiting a chance to move in and take over our lives. I didn't really understand what was meant by "takeover our lives" at the time but I was convinced even as a young child that it would mean that I would experience certain restrictions.

Our parents tried to teach us to recognize when the government was unfairly creating rules that would restrict our freedom. My mother homeschooled us — at the insistence of our grandparents — because she told us that we needed to learn critical thinking. She said that it would prevent us from being easily fooled by the government and would allow us to remain free. At the time, I didn't feel that I was restricted in any way except by my parents and their rules. We weren't allowed to talk to strangers, spend nights with our friends away from home, nor were we allowed to eat as much candy as we wanted. I didn't always like their rules but as a child I couldn't imagine anything worse.

I began to notice around age fourteen that life around me had started to change. It was then that I began to understand what my grandparents and parents had been warning us about. I started noticing a number of people staying at home during the day instead of working. As we drove by people's homes or apartment complexes, I would see adults sitting outside in chairs on their porches or on their lawns. Some were talking with neighbors across their fences. I would ask my mother who these people were and how they could survive without money that a job would afford them. Although my mother was never judgmental of these people in her responses, she did warn that she was concerned that they may be becoming too dependent upon the government and that this was a mistake. As I listened closely to my mother's explanations, I heard a foreboding tone in her voice. It was as if she couldn't explain it well enough or fast enough for me to understand. I sensed that she wanted me to grasp what she was saying before it was too late.

Unfortunately, it became too late for our country a year later. My country had fallen asleep and it had been too late to wake it up. That was when the Regime had been voted in by the adults. My family had gathered around our television waiting for voting results to be announced. There was tension in the air with worried anticipation that the voting may not have gone well. For months, the adults in my family had been a part of the Independence Party that been warning people about the threat that the Regime would bring if they were voted in. They spent tireless nights calling people, walking the neighborhoods, and raising money for the Independence Party cause. They feared that although many people were against the Regime, there was a greater number that didn't mind having their lives dictated to. They were tired of having to worry about making money to support themselves. The Regime promised equal pay for all, free healthcare, free food, and living units for all as well. It had been a difficult argument as to why this was not a good thing. Most potential voters were convinced that "free" things were good. What they failed to understand is that "free" things aren't free at all. They usually come at a high price. This time they would come at the high cost of our nation's freedom.

It had been a hard fought battle but the Independence Party had gone down in an absolute defeat. Members of the Independence Party, including my parents, began to be concerned about their safety following the election due to their outspokenness against the Regime. They were now being portrayed by the Regime as the ones fighting for Capitalism, and thus, inequality. They were the "greedy" ones who were against allowing everyone to be treated equally. Who but hate mongers would want to have such an unjust world where people worked to produce inequality rather than living their lives and being given equal treatment in all things? The Regime called for the immediate termination of the Independence Party, and it was cheered by those who had voted the Regime into office.

That's when change began to happen. Slowly at first, but then gradually the Regime had picked up speed in providing everything that all people in my country of Aplitacon needed. My country's name, once America, had been changed to the new name by the Regime, who believed that America was a name that represented a country of unequal and dominating classes over those less fortunate. Now, the new name, Aplitacon, would represent a new beginning of equality for all. The name was chosen by the leader of the Regime, Frederick A. Aplitacon. Apparently, we were to believe that his name symbolized everything that was "just."

It became clear very quickly that those in the Independence Party were not included in this equal treatment. Subsequent to the swearing-in of the Regime, those in the Independence Party who were known members were rounded up and taken to a central location where they could be retrained. My parents and grandparents were among those taken away. I had just turned seventeen years old. It was then that my two younger siblings and I were sent to live with a family that had agreed to take us in while our parents and grandparents received the necessary "training" to align their thinking with the new Establishment.

The couple and their young son seemed nice enough. They treated us all the same. We were given a room to share when it was decided that we didn't require anything more. Apparently, the Regime had issued a notification to families that all children of the same sex should share one room so as not to take more than they needed. Thus, my sisters and I shared one room with three identical-size beds. These beds had the same issued bedding, as well. We ate three meals a day and were required to attend the Regime's schools.

The Regime's school was far different than the teaching we had received from our mother. No longer were we able to study a variety of subjects or to have discussions about what we were learning. We were now given pages of information to memorize in three subjects only: math, spelling, and reading. Our subjects were bland and no debating was allowed. We were given the same number of pages to memorize and then a test was given. If we failed the test we were required to continue memorizing the subjects until we had mastered them. We finished school when it was decided by the teachers appointed by the Regime that we had reached our learning capacity. Some kids never made it past the sixth grade because they had reached their learning capacity, according to the teachers. The

Regime said that education wasn't important anyway because work was not a for-profit profession the way it had been. It was only necessary that enough work was done so that everyone could benefit by what was produced. A surplus of money or goods wasn't regarded as necessary by the Regime.

It became obvious to me that not much time was spent on the production of anything in the new country of Aplitacon. Most people spent their days watching television. Many of the television shows had become geared toward fulfilling sexual fantasies of adults and reporting on how well the leaders of the Regime were interacting with other countries of the world. The children's shows had focused mainly on saving the environment. The goal, according to the Regime, was for everyone in the world to work together collectively to attain global peace and other collaborative achievements. This was something that people had wanted to realize for a long time. I remember my mother talking about this during one of our homeschool history lessons and I heard many conversations on this topic when I was growing up. So many activists on television talked of how wrong wars were and how peace could be achieved if only the evil countries would give up their power and dominance over the world's "lesser" countries. It seemed now that Aplitacon was striving to set the example for the rest of the global collective to follow.

The more time that went by the more it became apparent that setting the example would also come at a high price. We were beginning to lose our need for money because all was provided by the Regime. While we should have felt good about our "equality" according to the Regime, we began to experience more sadness. Gone was the joy that had been experienced from working to reach personal goals. There was no more real "working together" or even working "by ourselves" to do anything. We didn't really need to work and most people chose not to, either because they had given up trying to change things or decided that a handout was better.

CHAPTER 6:
THE POINT OF NO RETURN

I had started to experience more and more sadness in my life as I progressed through my early adulthood under the laws established by the Regime. I vividly remember the depth of this sadness on the day I was finally allowed to visit my parents when I turned eighteen. It was hoped that since I was now an adult that I could assist them in giving up on their outdated and useless ideas of holding on to the world they once knew and the Independence Party in which they once placed their hope.

Thinking back, I recall that it had rained the night before and earlier that morning. I had been hoping that the weather would clear up so that I wouldn't get rained on when I was walking to the bus stop for the ride to the hospital. Mass transit was the preferred method of travel "suggested" by the Regime. Driving there in a car was highly frowned upon by the Regime, even if you were able to afford a car with its high price tag and high gas prices. The only people who needed to use a car, the Regime had declared, were those people in the government or those working on behalf of the government. In other words, the Regime and their friends were allowed privileges that others outside of the government were not afforded. Everyone seemed to take this disparity in treatment in stride.

I had thought about riding my bicycle. Riding a bicycle was acceptable to the Regime because bikes weren't considered a pollutant to the environment. However, today I was uncertain about the condition of the roads due to the rain and I wanted to make sure I arrived safely at the hospital to see my parents.

I had eaten lunch a couple of hours before getting ready to go. I remember anxiously awaiting the time that I was to leave for the hospital and being relieved when it finally came. I had dressed quickly in a nice pair of blue jeans, a white cotton short-sleeved blouse with buttons, and took along a light blue sweater in the event it got a little chilly later on. Early spring could bring uncertainty in the weather. I didn't realize then that as an adult I would consider a sweater a luxury item, due to living outside during the changes of season with little more than an old sleeping bag to keep me warm.

I had taken one last look in the mirror to ensure that I looked presentable enough for my parents. I anticipated hearing my mother say, "You have lost weight. Haven't you been eating?" My mother always thought I needed to eat more. I was medium build and a good weight for my average frame but my mother never thought I ate enough. She loved to cook and bake and always thought everyone could stand to gain a few pounds.

My father, on the other hand, never had a complaint. He would look at me when I was a young girl and say, "Sweetie, you are such a pretty girl. You are just perfect."

I would smile and give him a bear hug before returning to playing or homework. He would give me a little wink and tell me that he loved me. Those had been great memories of my parents and their love for me.

I remember, even then, catching the reflection of myself staring in the mirror lost in my childhood memories as I so often find myself today. I knew that I would need to stop dreaming and hurry if I didn't want to miss my bus. I had found the bus schedule online a couple of days ago and knew that the bus stop was approximately a quarter mile away. I knew I could run there if I needed to in order to be on time. It had gotten late and I realized I needed to hurry.

There had been no one home that day to say goodbye to or to ask about my appearance. The couple who had taken us in, Arlene and Jim, were not at home. They were out doing some community service work of some kind. I hadn't known for sure exactly what they did but I knew it involved pruning roses at the local community park. They told me that it was important to take care of flowers because they were an important part of the earth and good for the environment. I usually just nodded my head in agreement because I didn't want to discuss environmental issues with them. I had learned over time that any discussion regarding the environment could last for hours.

"Bethany, you and your sisters are going to need to become more involved in taking care of the environment," Arlene would say.

"I know your parents didn't teach you this, so now it's our responsibility to teach you to become a responsible member of the Regime's pro-environmental campaign."

That's when my sisters and I had been enrolled in our school's community program aptly named the Protectors of the Environment - The Youth of Aplitacon (PEYA). Each of us was given a shovel, gloves, and a burlap sack to use. We were not allowed to put waste materials in a plastic bag. All of the waste material gathered from the side of the road, in our yards, our neighbors' yards, and even our own, were to be placed in the more environmentally-friendly burlap sack.

We were given a telephone number to call when we observed environmental violations that were too big to place in our sack. We were encouraged to turn in our neighbors, our parents, our schools, businesses, or anyone else that we felt might be a "threat" to the environment in some way. The Regime investigated all complaints received by PEYA. Many families had been torn apart when some of the disgruntled youth figured out that their parents would not be able to defend themselves against the Regime if a complaint was filed for environmental abuses. Parents found in violation were removed temporarily from their homes until they promised to be better stewards of the environment. The youth began to realize that they had the upper hand over their parents without fear of consequence because their parents' authority had been nullified by the Regime's actions.

I left the house that morning on my way to the hospital and made it to the bus stop just in time to see the bus coming up the road. I had run part of the way and walked quickly the rest of the way. When I arrived at the bus stop, there were only two other people there waiting, an older man and woman who appeared to be a couple. The natural gas-propelled bus pulled up and opened its doors to allow passengers to board. There were no passengers getting off at our stop. In fact, once I boarded the bus I noticed that there was only one elderly man in his seventies, sitting by himself about halfway back. He was reading something and didn't look up as I took a seat three rows in front of him.

The bus ride to the hospital had been approximately three miles away. I was thankful that it had not been a longer trip. The bus driver, a heavyset man, who amply filled up the driver's seat, seemed irritated. Although, I couldn't make out every word he was saying, I could tell by his conversation with the older couple that he was upset because not enough people were riding the bus.

He said, "Just because it's Saturday doesn't mean that you can't ride the bus."

"More people need to take the bus so that fuel won't be wasted on a few. It's bad for our environment," he remarked.

Talk of the environment had been everywhere. It was the main topic of conversation wherever you went. I had chuckled and thought to myself as he spoke that perhaps no one was taking the bus because they didn't want to hear his complaints. The bus jolted a bit as the bus driver hit the brakes rather hard when he realized he was about to run over a pothole in the road. It seemed that repairing potholes, and the streets in general, had not been a priority for the Regime after the election. At least, it wasn't a priority to repair the roads in those sections of town that the Regime didn't frequent.

It had been late afternoon when I arrived at the Regime Hospital. I thought back about the hospital and what it had been used for before the Regime claimed it by eminent domain for its use. It had once stood as a thriving and patient-focused organization before the election. It had become merely a housing unit of sorts for those found in noncompliance with leadership's principles.

I was informed upon my arrival that my father and mother, along with my grandparents, had been separated when they were brought there. The women were housed together on the lower floors while the men were placed on the upper floors, I was told. This seemed odd to me since my parents and grandparents were married. Never in my lifetime had I heard of a government intervention that would allow for this type of housing separation away from the general public, let alone separating married couples from each other. At least, I had not heard of anything similar since hearing about the various camps set up during World War II after the bombing of Pearl Harbor or the concentration camps of Germany. No one really talked about the Regime Hospital on television anymore either. It seemed that following the Regime election and the initial coverage given about the demise of the shortsightedness of the Independence Party, all had fallen silent in the media.

I was escorted to a visitor waiting area by an attendee of the hospital. She was a relatively short woman in her early twenties with light brown hair who seemed pleasant enough, although she didn't make small talk. She was interested in getting back to watching television in the employee lounge. She had informed me that her favorite Regime show about a time of "waste" in America was coming on soon. She told me that she thought seeing how people used to live in America was so comical yet tragic at the same time. She said the show was about ancient history, during a time when men used to kill Native Americans for sport. She mentioned the name of the show as being about a man she called Dan L. Boone. I realized that she was talking about "Daniel Boone" and that she knew nothing about the history that she was referring. I thought about correcting her but I felt at the time that it wasn't worth the lengthy discussion that could delay my seeing my parents even further. I had not seen them in almost a year. I hadn't wanted any more delays.

The windowless visitor waiting room had been small and decorated with only the essentials. There were several gray thinly-cushioned chairs, a gray cushioned couch, and two steel end tables. Each end table held a coordinated steel lamp covered by a plain white lampshade, paper-thin but functional. The only decorations in the room were several Regime posters listing the locations of Regime Handout Centers. This was valuable information for anyone wanting to stock up if they were low on food or other items sanctioned by the Regime.

I remember I sat quietly waiting on the edge of one of the chairs. I thought several times that someone was coming to take me to see my parents but it was only other visitors milling about down the hall. I wasn't sure where I would be taken first. I wanted to see my mother but I was also anxious to see my father. I wondered what they would look like. How had they been treated? A year had been a long time for me with no communication allowed with my parents.

I had remembered my father telling us once when we were small that Christmas was only a year away. At the time, a year seemed like a lifetime. My father had said that a year seemed longer to children than it did to adults. I had never questioned his logic until sitting there in the visitor waiting room. It had seemed like an eternity before someone came to take me to see my parents. However, the years before my parents had been taken away now seemed to have flown by when I think back on it.

A young man, in his late twenties with short auburn hair and a pencil-thin moustache, appeared in the doorway of the waiting room. He was wearing his government-issued all-white uniform with matching white shoes. Nothing more was needed for a sterile hospital environment, I supposed. My thoughts were interrupted when he called my name. I had responded by rising quickly.

"I'm going to take you to see your father, Mr. Stimmick," he informed me. "Did anyone else come with you today?" he asked.

"No," I responded, thinking the question was somewhat unusual but I sloughed it off as meaningless.

I had started to tell him that I wanted to see my mother first, but thought better of it and just followed behind him in silence.

We had taken the elevator to the seventh floor. We exited after the short ride up and waited at the desk for permission to proceed on to my father's room. Several staff members also dressed in white were sitting behind the desk looking over what appeared to be patient charts. Each chart was in a square metal container that could only be opened inserting a flat key into the left side of the container.

Intermittently, the staff would stop to watch what was on the television screen mounted on the wall behind the desk. I could hear them talking to each other periodically about the news and how great things were these days now that the Regime was in charge.

The man I was with asked if my father was ready to receive a visitor. One of the older male staff members sitting behind the desk grunted a soft "yes" before returning to the review of his patient chart.

We made our way down the hall in silence. The young man was walking rather quickly now down the long white hallway. It struck me as we walked that there were no pictures on the wall. The walls were painted a sterile white; apparently pictures held no significance. The floors appeared more of a dingy white in color, most likely due to heavy foot traffic throughout many days and nights. We finally reached room 713. The young man stopped so suddenly that I almost plowed into the back of him before I realized that this was our destination.

He had turned to look at me accusingly and then changed his mind before making an insulting remark at my carelessness. I could tell that I was taking up too much of his time now by the exasperated look on his face. He seemed as though he were bored with the whole "visitor guide" routine and just wanted to return to what he was doing before I had interrupted his day.

"This is the room you want," he indicated. "You won't be able to stay long. Make the most of your time because it's getting near dinner. Visitors aren't allowed to have dinner with the patients."

"But I wanted to see my mother, too," I cried out before realizing I had become emotional.

"Well, you'll just have to come back another day. It won't happen today."

With that he turned abruptly on his heels and scurried down the hall, leaving me alone in front of my father's door.

CHAPTER 7:
MY FATHER'S EYES

I remember I had tried to put aside my frustration before opening the door to my father's room. The young man escorting me had been rude but I hadn't wanted to let that put a damper on the reunion with my father. As I had begun to push the door to go in, I could hear a faint voice in the background. My father must be watching television I thought, or perhaps a staff member was helping him get ready for dinner.

I had pushed the door with a little more force the second time, and could see that my father was alone in his room. The room was the familiar old-style hospital room that used to be so prevalent before the Regime. There was a single bed that had been pushed up against the room's only window. The window was about the size of an average door. However, the windowpane was made of etched glass, which made it impossible to see outside. The room was dimly lit and I had barely been able to make out an overstuffed chair that was placed next to the bed. I don't know what I had expected to see but I thought there would be more in the room. I thought my father would have a place to store his food, a television, an eating area, and a separate living space. After all, that's what all of the living units were given since the Regime took office. Why was my father's room different from everyone else's? That didn't seem in line with the Regime's philosophy.

As I moved closer, I saw that my father was sitting on the edge of his small bed. It was what used to be considered a hospital bed in the old days. My father had been dressed in what appeared to be an old-fashioned hospital gown, as well. It was the kind that opens in the back exposing one's backside to everyone right before you lose all of your dignity, I had thought to myself. Once you turn away from a visitor forgetting that there is a gaping hole in the back of your gown, you can never regain the dignity that you once possessed. I always felt those gowns were just awful for the ego.

As I stood there in my father's hospital room, I had let my mind wander back to the time I saw my grandmother wearing one of those gowns when I went to visit her in a hospital. She had fallen ill one day and was taken by ambulance to the emergency room. It had all happened so suddenly.

It had started with a dream I had one night about my grandfather. It had seemed that he was trying to tell me something but I woke up just as he began to speak. I knew that my grandfather was on a short trip visiting his sister and wasn't at home. That meant that my grandmother was home alone. The dream had been a little disheartening. I couldn't really make out what it had been about but I awoke with a feeling of urgency. I knew that I needed to call my mother because I feared that something was dreadfully wrong with my grandmother.

I reached my mother while she was at work. My mother worked in a local bakery and was the assistant manager. She came to the phone after what seemed to be a very long time. It was actually less than three minutes that I had been waiting. During this time, I could hear the baking sheets slapping against the large metal sinks in the background. People were laughing and talking to each other. I couldn't clearly make out all of the conversations but I could hear words about how much flour was needed and who was going to wash the next pans that would soon be coming out of the large ovens. People enjoyed working at the bakery and my mother enjoyed her job there as well.

My mother had answered with her usual cheerful, "Hello."

"Mom," I said with sharp tone to my voice that must have frightened her a bit.

"Is everything ok?" she asked.

I had quickly told my mother about the dream that I had experienced the night before regarding my grandmother. I told her that I was concerned that something had happened to her. I tried to explain why I felt this way but was unable to pinpoint the reason. My mother tried to calm my fears by telling me that my grandmother was fine and that she had seen her only a couple of hours ago before leaving for work.

My grandmother was in her sixties at the time and no longer worked. She had retired after working all of her life in the bakery. In fact, it had been my grandmother that had taught my mother everything that she knew about baking cakes, cookies, pies, and an assortment of other baked goods. They would spend hours working with each other trying to create masterpieces for the customers. Each cake or baked good was made with an expression of love. Both my mother and grandmother would bake each item as though they were making it for their own family. They aimed for perfection so that each bite would be savored. Only then would my mother and grandmother feel that they had accomplished what they had set out to do. They enjoyed their work because they saw the smiles of approval on their customers' faces. They had so much repeat business from happy clients that the owner of the bakery more or less let them run everything. He was pleased that he had two people who may have loved the bakery more than he did.

I remember spending hours there watching my mother and grandmother painstakingly decorate cakes. The bakery was permanently filled with the sight and smells of cake dough, flour, chocolate cookies, and every dessert imaginable. I marveled at how they seemed to effortlessly know the ingredients that were required for each dessert. I wondered how they knew this. What I didn't know was the hours they spent learning their craft and mastering it with pride.

Thinking back now on those days, I wish I had paid more attention to the details. I regret not listening more closely to the conversations they had about how to make a certain dessert and why it was important to get it just right.

"Barbara," my grandmother would snap. "You need to measure that better," referring to the flour and baking soda my mother would put into a large stainless steel mixing bowl.

"That's not enough flour and baking soda. The cake won't rise properly."

"Mom, I know what I'm doing," my mother would retort.

"I know your great-grandmother's recipe better than you do, Barbara. Now don't argue with me. I would hate for you to have to start all over again."

My mother, knowing that she wouldn't win any argument about baking, especially when it involved her great-grandmother's cake recipe, would silently surrender the fight. She allowed her mother to dictate the remaining ingredients.

My mother would just smile and shake her head as she would jokingly ask my grandmother, "Are you going to tell the customers how to eat the cake too?"

Theirs was an art that had been forever lost. No longer did the workers of today seem to care about such trivialities. Food was food. You didn't need to play with it to make it special. You just had to eat it. Besides that, all of the cooking and baking time just wasn't good for the environment anyway. Just ask the Regime. They would give you several explanations as to why cooking and baking by many businesses throughout the country was so harmful to the collective.

My mother had hung up from our conversation after telling me again not to worry about my grandmother. She promised that she would call her the first chance she got. She reiterated that she would be fine. However, that wouldn't be the case.

My mother would later recount that day when she tried calling my grandmother during her first break but there was no answer. My mother decided that she was probably just outside or napping. Not to worry. She would try to reach her later on. My mother tried calling my grandmother a second time during her lunch break. When my grandmother didn't answer this time, my mother became worried. She tried a couple of more times without success.

My mother ran to find the store owner. She told him that she thought something may be wrong with her mother and that she needed to run home to find out. He assured her that it was okay to leave.

When my mother arrived she found the front door locked. She initially knocked on the door but there was no response. She used her key to go inside the house. As she slipped the key in and turned the knob, she found my grandmother unconscious on the living room floor. She immediately called an ambulance and my grandmother was taken to the emergency room. Grandmother spent the next week in intensive care as they tried to determine what was wrong with her. The doctors finally discovered that it was her gall bladder and removed it immediately. My mother was later told that if she hadn't found my grandmother when she did that she would have died. As I sat next to my grandmother in the hospital room later that week, I was grateful for the dream that I had. As I watched my mother help my grandmother close the back of her hospital gown as a new visitor came into the room, I was reminded of just how fragile both our life and our dignity are.

My father hadn't seemed to notice that I had been standing in the same place for a few moments in his hospital room caught up in the memories of my grandmother. I was the one who had noticed that I hadn't moved in quite some time. I walked over to where he was sitting. It was then that I could see his lips moving. He was mumbling something that I couldn't quite make out. I looked around for the light switch but couldn't find one.

I had called out his name but he didn't respond to me. It was as though he was lost in thought, unable to detect anything around him. I inched closer, concerned now that something was wrong.

I said, "Father?" a little louder this time.

He stopped mumbling but didn't look up. I then looked over to my right and saw a small table lamp on a nightstand next to his bed. I reached to turn it on and fumbled to find the switch. I finally found it and remember the room brightened a little as it turned on. The bulb had been a low-watt bulb. One that was more environmentally friendly. That was an important lesson that the Regime wanted everyone to learn. The environment, the school children were taught, is your friend.

"Neither you nor your parents have a right to destroy the environment by being selfish," I recall hearing in one of the Regime's many speeches on the environment.

I remember my sisters had come home from hearing the speech and denounced our parents because of what they had not taught us in homeschool. They said they never realized how horrible our parents had been in using high-wattage bulbs in our house. They vowed never to treat the environment as poorly as our parents. It changed their once loving perception of our parents that day. Our "new parents," the ones that had taken us in when our parents had been taken, were now viewed as perfect because they acknowledged that the environment was sacred.

Again, I called out to my father. This time he looked up and answered.

"Who's there?"

"Daddy it's me."

He began to laugh. He immediately stood up and began to pace around the room.

"You know what? I played basketball last night with a couple of young guys on the floor. They thought they could take this old man down but they were wrong. They won't try something that stupid again. Better not doubt me. I'll beat their asses."

Shocked by what I was witnessing, I watched quietly for a few minutes as my father paced back and forth in the room. I had never seen him like this nor had I ever heard him use such language.

Not once did he acknowledge who I was or ask why I was there. He didn't even seem to realize that it had been over a year since we had last seen each other. He just kept walking about, making movements as though he were bouncing a basketball on the floor and then throwing the imaginary ball into an imaginary hoop. I was spellbound for a few minutes, unable to comprehend what was happening. This wasn't the man that I remembered as my father. This was a stranger that I had never met.

My father continued to walk around the room talking about the basketball game he had played while becoming more and more agitated with every breath. I had known that I needed to calm him down before he could have a heart attack. His eyes had become glassy and it seemed that he wasn't able to focus on reality. Just when I was reaching for his arm, a hospital staff member came in and ordered my father to sit down. He was an older man that I think I may have seen sitting behind the desk when I came in. He was a tall man in his early forties. His temples were graying and he walked with a slight limp in his right leg. He was direct in his tone and this made my father abruptly stop his talking and pacing.

"Sit down over here," he shouted as he motioned my father to his bed.

My father had quickly run to the bed and jumped on top of it like a young boy who had been caught by his mother and scolded for doing something wrong. I could only watch in disbelief as my father seemed unable to defend himself. I had never heard anyone ordering my father around like that. My father would never have allowed someone to treat him with such disrespect.

The man turned to look at me and said, "I think it's best you leave now. It's almost time for dinner and I have to get him ready to go to the dining room."

I recall starting to say something but the man had taken my father by his left arm and had begun pulling him along toward the bathroom, presumably to wash up before dinner. As I turned to leave the room, I tripped over a small square-shaped table that I had not seen when I entered the room. The sting of the steel against my knee made me pause momentarily to grab my knee. I felt the rush of blood moving slowly up my leg, the pain burning as it climbed up toward my thigh. I winced but I wasn't sure at that moment which hurt more, the pain from my knee hitting the table that would most likely leave a temporary bruise on my skin or the pain of seeing a man who used to be my father that would forever leave a scar on my heart.

I had left the room with my head spinning that day. I wanted to run and also to stay all at the same time. I remember thinking to myself that I wanted my childhood back. None of my thoughts had given me much comfort. I knew I had to find out what had happened to the father that I once knew. I had known that this wasn't him.

CHAPTER 8:
OUR RISE AND FALL

Once outside my father's room, I remember that I ran back down the hall using the wall to maintain my balance. I felt sick to my stomach and needed the wall just to hold me up. I reached the desk and tried to catch my breath before speaking. No one looked up at me. It was as if they were used to most of their visitors reacting the way I did. Had they seen this all before or was it that they just stopped caring about anything except themselves?

"Excuse me." I interrupted the reading of patient charts and the watching of television.

One of the staff members slowly looked up, disinterested but obliged to respond.

"Yes, what do you need?" he asked.

"I need to speak with someone concerning my father," I said, adding emphasis to the word "need."

"You mean room 713?"

"Yes, my father. What has happened to him?"

"What do you mean?" he asked.

"My father is acting different than when I last saw him."

"Maybe it's just been a while," he sarcastically remarked.

"No," I said, a little more sternly then I had intended. "He's not the same."

"Let me pull his chart and I'll see what I can find."

He had moved from his chair and proceeded slowly to the charts that were located on shelves on the back wall. He thumbed seemingly through every file. I couldn't tell from where I was standing if the files were in alphabetical order or listed by room. It seemed that whatever the case was he was having a hard time understanding the system because it took a long time.

Occasionally, he would stop to talk to another staffer about something they had just seen on the television. He laughed at an old sitcom about Jackie Gleason. I heard him say how strange it was that someone would work so hard at driving a bus around all day taking people from one stop to another. He also remarked that it couldn't have been "healthy" for the environment to use all of that fuel and pollute the air on a daily basis as Jackie Gleason's character had done. As he stood shaking his head at the stupidity of it all, I couldn't help but wonder when it had all changed.

Had it really just changed with the Regime, I remember thinking? Could you really change the way people viewed things overnight or did it take longer? It seemed to me that it was a gradual process.

I recall listening to my grandmother and grandfather talk about their childhood memories. They discussed how their parents had worked such long hours to put food on their table. They spoke of a time called The Great Depression, when people who had been hard workers suddenly found themselves out of work and standing in food lines just to get scraps to feed their children. It had made me feel proud of my relatives, some that I had never known, who sacrificed for themselves and others in order to have a better life, a life where they were free to create, a life that enabled them to buy what they wanted, and to give to others in need so that they could reach their individual full potential. I had watched my own parents working hard to provide for their three children. My mother working long hours in the bakery every day while my father worked nights as a nurse's aide in the same hospital that he was now "imprisoned" in.

I watched some, however, in my parents' generation begin to shift the way they viewed work. There seemed to be more and more people that my parents would discuss that just didn't try to find employment. I remember them sitting around the kitchen table while my sisters and I played in the living room adjacent to them. They would talk about the family down the street and how the father drank heavily, rendering him unable to provide for his family. I had learned information in my childhood that would become useful to me later in adulthood.

Growing up, I would hear my own age group talking about how they wanted to "get rich quick." I heard adults asking kids in church or elsewhere what they wanted to be when they grew up. As a young child, the answers would be something like a doctor, a nurse, or a fireman. This was soon replaced in my later years by a singer, an environmentalist, or a star. I never understood those responses. While creative, none of those careers seemed to require the same hard work that my parents, my grandparents, and my grandparents' parents had endured. It seemed more acceptable to pursue whatever your heart desired whether or not it would earn you money. If you didn't earn money then you could always fall back on your parents. Parents had been raised by their parents to expect to have to work hard to earn a living. You didn't have to choose to be that way as a young adult if you didn't want to be. At least that had become the acceptable solution to most.

My parents tried to shield us from such ideologies. I now believe that is the main reason that they felt that homeschooling was so important. They wanted to raise us with their values. Until recently, that had worked. But even my sisters now felt that my parents had been wrong in their beliefs. They felt that my parents had been traitors to the environment and a better way of life, a life where no one "had" to work. Work was considered something you chose to do so that you could help out by contributing to the betterment of the whole. You worked not to get paid, but to help out. The goal was to assist the Regime in carrying out their goals for the betterment of the collective. These goals were geared toward protecting the environment, making sure everyone else did as well, and collectively assuring that everyone in the country received the same as every other person.

I wondered that day, while visiting my father in the hospital, why the Regime's goals had not been followed where he was concerned. As I watched the staff member continue to try and locate my father's chart, I kept thinking why was my father being treated as if he didn't have a say in anything? Just as I was about to continue this line of thinking, the staff member interrupted me by clearing his throat and looking at me as if I was taking up too much of his time.

"I found your father's chart. Do you want me to look at it?"

I looked up at him, trying to hide the distain that I felt for him at that moment. "Please," I managed to say almost politely.

"It says here that your father experienced some sort of mental breakdown."

"He had a mental breakdown? What do you mean?"

"Just what I said," he retorted loudly. "He apparently was taken off some medication that he was prescribed and then he just snapped. It happens. I've seen it a few times."

"Well, is there anything that can help him? How long will he be this way?" I asked.

"Unfortunately, once that happens it's usually not something you can come back from."

His words had been cut off by his own laughter and the laughter coming from the other staff members. It seemed that Jackie Gleason had just told his best friend Norman that he was angry with him for getting on his nerves. While I could relate to the getting on the nerves part, I didn't understand why in the middle of a serious conversation this man took time to laugh at something on television. Where was the sympathy for a man's daughter who had just discovered that the man she knew as her father no longer existed?

I turned to walk away when the staff member called after me.

"Miss, miss," he said, "Is there anything else you're in need of?"

There's that word "need" again, I had thought.

Yes, I had needed something. I had needed this man to treat me like a human being who had just lost her father, I thought to myself.

I hadn't responded, however, but kept on walking quickly toward the elevator. Thankfully, someone was just exiting the elevator so that I easily walked in and escaped from the world that existed inside the hospital.

On my way out of the hospital I thought, what would my mother be like when I found her? Would she be "gone" like my father? Had she even been told what had happened to my father? It was all too much for me to handle at that moment. I just wanted to retreat into my bed back at my "home." The environmentally-inspired home with its environmentally-conscious occupants, I had scoffed to myself. Tonight, that "home" would have to do, I remember thinking.

CHAPTER 9:
GRANDPA

I had found myself alone in my bedroom the next morning after visiting my father. It was a room that I normally shared with my two younger sisters. They were customarily early risers so it was no surprise that they were already up before me.

Thinking back, I remember longing for the days when we each had our own room. Privacy was at a surplus then. Privacy, however, had become something that was frowned upon because it seemed that the Regime considered "using more than you needed" as yet another waste. The Regime had encouraged the downsizing of everything, from food to cars to housing. "No one needs to have more than they really need" was their slogan printed on numerous billboards and shown in commercials on television. Not well written perhaps, but effective and to the point nonetheless. Maybe some people just want it, I had thought to myself, as I lay awake aching for better times. It was the Regime, however, who decided what we needed. That was something we no longer "needed" to do for ourselves.

The morning sunlight had begun to creep in through the bedroom window and shine onto the foot of my bed as I lay there. Soon, I knew that it would be making its way up to the top of my bed and eventually shine directly in my eyes. I had thought about closing the blinds but believed it would be a waste of energy. I remember thinking, the sun after all was something to be worshipped and shared by everybody. We were to respect the sun and the warmth it provided. At least, that's what the Regime had taught the younger children in their schools.

I recall feeling myself becoming more cynical each day. My cynicism had begun to rob me of what little joy I still possessed. Maybe I had a right to feel cynical, I thought to myself as I lay there. After all, I had sobbed into my pillow most of the night after returning from seeing my father in the Regime Hospital. I knew that I would never forget what they had done to him. He was no longer someone that I recognized.

I had felt lost and alone lying there on my bed. I hadn't cried that much since I witnessed the passing of my grandfather before the Regime had been elected. The memory of his passing made a profound impact on my life.

My grandmother had married my grandfather when she was a mere fourteen years old. She would sit and talk for hours about the young nineteen-year-old that she had fallen so deeply in love with and married. During my grandmother's day and age, marrying young was not frowned upon. In fact, it was encouraged. Since technology and medicine wasn't as advanced then, death came early for most. The average age that people attained back then was about fifty to sixty years old. Starting a family had to be done early so that time wouldn't run out before minor children were left parentless.

My grandfather, according to my grandmother, was a great family man. He worked hard at the bakery alongside my mother and grandmother. It would be years after his passing that my grandmother would remarry. I think she remarried out of necessity and not so much out of love. She cared for her current husband, but I don't think she ever found her heart again after my grandfather died.

My grandfather was a nurturer by nature. He typically raised a garden every year during his time off from the bakery. He wanted to make sure that he provided well for his family.

I remember having a conversation with him shortly before he passed away. I had walked outside one late afternoon to find him. I wanted to talk to him and spend some time together, just the two of us. He always shared stories about his childhood and gave me encouragement about being able to do whatever I wanted to do in life if I was willing to work for it.

I searched unsuccessfully for him around the yard for what seemed like a long time. I became concerned that it was getting late and I wouldn't be able to find him before it got dark. Suddenly, across the yard and out in the garden I caught a glimpse of my grandfather. He was bent over near the ground, straightening out the row of green leafed vegetables that he had recently planted. He had already planted another row adjacent to that one, which was already producing the yellowest corn that I had ever seen.

My grandmother used to say, "Your grandfather has the greenest thumb of anyone I've ever known."

She was right. He produced so much food in the garden that we ended up giving much of it away to friends and neighbors. This still allowed us to be able to eat what we wanted and to freeze the rest of our food in a large freezer that we kept in the garage.

The Regime didn't allow freezers after their election. They explained that extra food was not a necessity. They indicated that food was provided for all people equally and that no one should have more than anyone else. We were rationed food on a weekly basis.

I remember this "rationing process" very well. My "new" parents, who had become our caretakers while our parents were in the Regime's hospital, had us line up with them in the center of town at a pre-selected time designated to us by the Regime. The Regime mailed a postcard to each family at the beginning of the month noting the time and date they were to collect their food.

We stood in front of a huge gray warehouse along with hundreds of other people until it was our turn to enter. When directed to do so, we would hand over our postcard in exchange for three medium-sized bags of food that had been pre-packaged. What we were given varied sometimes, but mostly it consisted of meat, potatoes, some fruit, and some other canned items. Each person in line was given exactly the same food and the same amount. No one complained but accepted what was allowed them. I had only seen one person complain in all the time that we had been coming to the warehouse.

I remember that day well because it was a particularly hot day. We arrived at our scheduled time close to eleven thirty in the morning. It was already getting warm by then because it was mid-July. We were not provided water or chairs when we stood in line. It was explained that chairs and water weren't necessary if you were keeping yourself in good shape and drinking the daily amount of water provided.

However, people were on edge because the sun was hotter than usual that day. Some people in line started to grumble about others standing too close to them. The line would suddenly lurch forward on occasion when a shove from a teenager would send another teenager falling to the ground. After someone reminded the teen that his behavior was unacceptable, the line would quiet down again and everyone would settle back into their respective place in line.

Our wait wasn't usually that long. However, for some reason that day the line seemed to move slower than normal. One man who appeared to be in his forties and standing near us began to complain about the wait.

He was a tall man and stood out above most in the line. He was wearing a green t-shirt with a logo on the front that represented his support of the Regime's Media Network. The logo showed the letters RMN above a cheering crowd gathered around a man holding a microphone with the letters RMN prominently displayed on it. It was what you saw on billboards and television commercials day and night. The media's report was always pro-Regime. It seemed that the Regime could do no wrong in their eyes.

The man's voice grew louder and the complaints became more easily recognizable. He complained about having to wait in the long line and not being able to choose what he wanted to eat. At first I thought I was hearing things. I'd never heard anyone complain about the Regime since the Independence Party tried to warn everyone before the election about the proposed new government ideologies. This was unheard of. Several people in the line tried to get the man to stop talking. However, that just seemed to provoke him and make matters worse. His tone of voice became increasingly loud.

I watched as a couple of people left the line and entered the warehouse. I wasn't sure where they were going. I thought perhaps they were trying to cut in line since no one was paying attention, but then that was against the Regime's rules. The Regime had pointed out that no one ever needed to "take" something away from anyone else because everyone had been given the same of everything.

Moments later I saw why the people had left the line. They had gone to get the Regime so that they could handle the situation. No one knew how to handle the matter on their own.

Two male Regime staffers dressed in their weekday uniforms, consisting of black pants, black steel-toed shoes and long-sleeved dark gray shirts, hurriedly walked up to the gentleman and with what seemed like one precise motion, grabbed his arms on either side and quickly removed him from the line. The three disappeared quietly into a corner of the warehouse never to be seen again. I could see the panicked look on the man's face as he was dragged across the warehouse floor.

I looked all over the warehouse when it was our turn to go inside to retrieve our food rations. I saw other uniformed Regime staffers milling about the tables where the food was sitting but I never again saw a trace of the man or the Regime staffers who had taken him away. I would never find out what happened to him.

There had never been "food rationing" or frustrations about the limiting of food when my grandfather was alive and providing for us from his plentiful garden. What he couldn't grow in his garden he would buy at the grocery store. There were aisles and aisles of food for the choosing. There were always several varieties of anything that you wanted and there was no limit to what you could purchase.

I remember once asking my grandfather if we could grill some hot dogs. He ran through a variety of hot dog selections from pork to beef and Kosher to plain, asking me which one I wanted. At that time, there were several varieties and brand names from which to choose and I took it for granted that I had a choice.

There was no choice to be made after the Regime. The Regime packaged all food in containers that listed only the name of the item along with a label of the Regime logo, a Regime Food Products label or RFP. There was no description of the food listed on the side of the containers as there had been when my grandfather bought me hot dogs. There could have been any number of ingredients in our Regime food. The Regime explained the absence of the ingredients as merely a waste of effort to place such information on containers when they were aware of what was in the food. They knew what was nutritious and they would make the decision about what was best for us to consume. There was simply nothing to know beyond that!

I couldn't imagine that day, as I stood watching my grandfather tend to his garden, that life could become so dire after the Regime takeover. My grandfather looked up after a few more moments of digging in the earth with a small hand-held hoe. He smiled at me and asked how long I had been there in the garden. I told him that I had only been there for a few moments. He stood up and walked over to where I was standing.

He said, "It's good to see you honey" and gave me one of his gentle hugs that I had come to expect. His hugs always made me feel so safe.

His arms had closed tightly around my small shoulders. His flannel shirt pressed against my face had smelled of cherry-scented pipe tobacco and perspiration. His scent engulfed my nostrils with a familiar smell that reminded me of him and the comforts of home.

"What are you doing out here so late?" I asked.

"I'm just trying to get some work done so your grandmother won't have to worry about anything."

"What do you mean, Grandpa?"

"I just don't like the thought of your grandmother having to worry about buying food that I can grow. I feel better knowing that she has all she needs," he responded.

I had smiled at the thought of how much he loved my grandmother. You could see it in everything that he did. He thought more about what she wanted and needed rather than what he needed. He was a great example of the kind of man that I hoped to marry someday.

My grandfather leaned forward and took me by the hand. We walked slowly together back to the house. The sun had moved farther down into the sky. Night had been upon us.

I skipped and kicked at rocks on the path back to the house as we talked about how much corn, tomatoes, squash, and other vegetables that we would have to eat. I loved my grandfather so much.

At one point along the way, we stopped so he could catch his breath. My grandfather had been diagnosed years earlier with a heart condition. I noticed then that he had begun to take things more slowly.

It was then for the first time, that I looked up at him and said as well as any twelve-year-old girl could, "Grandpa, I love you."

He smiled lovingly back at me and told me that he loved me also. I didn't know it at the time, but it would be the last opportunity that I would ever get to tell him how I felt. My grandfather would die of a heart attack the very next day.

CHAPTER 10:
SAYING GOODBYE IS NEVER EASY

It was a day that started off seemingly a bit humid. The air was thick. The sun was sitting directly above in the bright blue May sky. It was late spring and the skies were usually clear with no clouds in sight. On that particular day, however, it looked as though it might rain. I remember seeing the large grayish white clouds forming at the base of the mountains as I looked outside of our living room window. I had learned in my childhood that it meant a thunderstorm was possibly coming.

It was always so beautiful watching the sun come up over the mountains from our big second-story windowsill. We lived in an old home with our grandparents at the time. The house was a two-story home that was over a hundred years old, according to my mother. It had been in the family for a long time and sat up on a hillside overlooking the main two-lane road below.

It was a house that reminded me of an old country farmhouse because it had been painted red at one point. My grandfather had added on to the house by building a stairway at the side of the house leading up to the balcony. It seemed that everyone loved sitting on the balcony. Having access to it by way of either the inside or outside of the house just made it more convenient for everyone to enjoy the balcony.

As a pre-teen I loved to run up and down the stairs for hours using them as part of a make-believe cruise ship stairway that led up to the ship's main deck or, in reality, our balcony. I would greet those relaxing on the "deck" and run to fetch them their favorite drink as part of the service provided by the cruise line. Those were simpler times when a kid could be a kid. They are memories that I like to hold on to when it gets hard to cope with the reality of things under the Regime.

I also recall sitting out on the balcony many times with my sisters and other family members. It was especially nice on afternoons or evenings when there was a light rain. You could hear the rain gently falling on the wooden roof that covered the balcony. The rain always brought with it a light cool breeze that swept through the balcony and past those who were enjoying the sounds, smells, and feel of an afternoon or evening shower.

We would sit for hours in chairs or on patio swings that rocked effortlessly back and forth, lulling us to sleep along with the rain. This would be the vantage point from where I would watch my grandfather fall to the ground and pass away. The balcony would never again have the same meaning of comfort that it once held. It was a painful memory that I could live without.

It was a Saturday. My grandfather had been in a hurry all day to mow the lawn. He wanted my grandmother to have a nice yard to look at when she sat on the balcony later that evening. He had gone to the gas station earlier in the morning to buy gas for the mower. The lawn mower had run out of gas the last time the grass was cut. It had never been replenished. Although, my grandfather was getting up in years, at seventy-two years of age he still felt that he was capable of doing anything. I think we all believed him.

He had wanted to mow the yard earlier but as was not uncommon in North Carolina during days of high humidity, an unexpected light rain shower had blown through dotting the ground with just enough moisture for my grandfather to have to wait until much later in the afternoon before mowing. It had gotten progressively hotter during the day and the grass was still damp, but that didn't stop him from following through with his plans.

Once the rain had stopped, several of us, including my grandmother, had moved to the balcony. It was hot in the house and the balcony would provide a welcome relief from the still air inside. My grandfather was just starting up the lawnmower as we took our seats.

The grass had grown thick over the last couple of weeks. It was going to be hard to mow the grass today because of its height, I thought to myself. Suddenly, within minutes of starting to mow the grass, my grandfather stood motionless for a few seconds and then fell down backwards onto the grass. The lawnmower still churned loudly as it stood motionless next to my grandfather. My grandmother called out frantically for my mother to help and then called out my grandfather's name seeking some kind of sign that he was okay.

My mother was the first to reach him as I stood helplessly watching it all unfold from the balcony. She immediately began trying to resuscitate my grandfather who now lay lifeless on the ground next to her. My mother screamed for someone to call an ambulance. I'm not sure who called but within minutes an ambulance came and took my grandfather away. My mother jumped into the ambulance to make the ride to the hospital with my grandfather in the hopes that his life would be saved.

My grandfather would be pronounced dead shortly thereafter. I would never again see him in the garden working to provide for his family, nor would I ever feel his embrace or smell the wonderful scents that only belonged to my grandfather. He was gone and my childhood had gone with him.

I would be left in a few years with the stark reality of a Regime who would not have appreciated the sentiment that I felt for my grandfather. He would have been considered a "less valuable" member of society due to his health and aging, and therefore, expendable for the good of the collective.

CHAPTER 11:
CHILD'S PLAY: A LOST ART

I realized that I had been sitting in one place for most of the morning thinking back yet again about my childhood and happier days. I had caught myself recently spending more and more time reminiscing about my childhood instead of staying centered on the harsher realities of the present day. I couldn't afford to disconnect too long, nor could I afford to stay in one place for very long. It wasn't safe.

I sat motionless for a moment afraid to move. Had I been seen? I looked around and could see a family of four walking through the park approximately fifty yards in front of me. It appeared to me to be a mother and father with two young children. I watched as the mother clothed in a loose-fitting yellow dress and white sweater bent down to tuck her son's shirt back in his pants. It appeared that this was something that she normally did often because as soon as she had his shirt tucked neatly back in it became loose when he ran around wildly chasing his sister.

I watched as the father helped the mother corral the children into the area next to where swings had once hung. The swings had been removed after the Regime was elected. The Regime had convinced most parents who voted for them that swinging was a dangerous activity that usually resulted in unnecessary injuries. Unnecessary injuries, the Regime concluded, resulted in a loss for the collective as a whole. This was something that the Regime wouldn't tolerate. They had convinced the public that preventing injuries was a duty of every citizen to the collective. According to the

Regime, no one should have to take care of someone else if it wasn't necessary. There would be no necessity if the activity were avoided altogether.

Parents had agreed that children could occupy themselves with other less accident-provoking activities such as hopscotch. Hopscotch was an old childhood game where kids drew nine blocks with chalk, usually on pavement. The squares produced a grid consisting of single and double squares. The goal was to toss a rock or a coin in the square that you wanted. You would then hop to the square next to where the coin lay and pick it up while poised on one leg. I think there was more to the game but I never really played it as a child. My mother enrolled us in softball, tennis, and other games that required more athletic involvement.

I continued to observe the family as they walked to the edge of the park. The parents kept interrupting their children's playtime when they would attempt to run around. Every time the children would start to run or jump up and down, one of the parents would direct the children to stop.

"Janie, I told you to stop running," the father said, rather abruptly. "You too Steve. Don't let me have to tell you kids again. You know you aren't allowed to run around like that."

The children reluctantly acquiesced to the commands given them after several attempts to change their parents' minds.

I remarked to myself at how different this had been from my childhood and watching these parents admonish their children for playing saddened me. Growing up in North Carolina in the mountains allowed for a great many fun adventures. The possibilities had been endless.

Having the woods as my backyard allowed for hours and hours of climbing trees, running unabashedly through the piles of leaves in the fall, and swinging from vines that were once connected to the tall trees. Most of the trees were oak or pine. There were plenty of pinecones and oak leaves scattered on the ground. We would collect the pinecones for hours and then use them as objects to throw at each other or at the neighborhood kids.

My sisters and I loved walking around in the woods. We played a game called "Tarzan and Jane," named for a television series about a man who lived in the jungle, scantily clothed in only a loin cloth, and a woman named Jane who fell in love with him. Tarzan used to swing from the trees or run through the jungle.

It seemed that I was always selected to be the Tarzan character since I was the oldest. I didn't mind because I was a tomboy of sorts. I would jump off of small boulders and run wildly through the woods in my best Tarzan impression while one of my sisters would play the damsel in distress named Jane. My other sister would be the villain, whose goal it was to hurt Jane in order to capture the jungle boy.

We would run and fall, jump up, and run and fall some more. At times, we would fall down on sticks or rocks buried just beneath the dirt. We would come home at times with cuts and bruises but thankfully never any broken bones.

Our bumps and bruises had been no big deal to us or to our mother. She would clean us up, bandage our cuts, kiss them and send us on our way back to conquer another adventure. It is a memory that I look back on with great affection. It was some of the most fun that I can ever remember having. It was something that these children, now walking quietly along in the park glued to their parents' sides, would never experience because it might be detrimental to the collective.

When had that changed? Why had many of these parents, who themselves had experienced a similar childhood as mine, allowed the Regime to take that happiness away from their own children? They had so readily given over control of their children's happiness to someone else because they were told they needed to do so.

That was one of the reasons that I had chosen to never have children. I had seen the drastic changes after the Regime took over and I knew that I didn't want them controlling my children's lives. My mother had worked too hard to give me freedom as a child for me to now willingly give up the freedom of my children to a government that believed children needed their leadership instead of the guidance of their parents.

My mother had always been the one to encourage us to "go outside and play," something that I hadn't heard parents tell their children since the Regime's reign began.   Parents today encouraged their children to stay inside. There was always television to watch. What more did a child need? The media constantly reminded parents of the hazards of outdoor playing and convinced them that they had made the right decision by keeping their children safely inside. The Regime knew what was best for children even if their parents disagreed. Not many disagreed, however, and those that did kept silent for fear of retribution.

CHAPTER 12:
REUNIONS

All the thinking I was doing about the old days when children could be children eventually brought up memories of my mother again. The woman I saw earlier in the park, walking with her husband and two small children, was similar in size and shape to my mother when she was taken from us by the Regime.

My mother was only 5'3" but she was a strong and robust woman. I don't believe that anyone ever realized that she was so short in stature. The way she carried herself so upright made everyone she came in contact with think that she was much taller. She was also very confident in herself. I think that helped to carry forth the illusion that my mother was a big presence. Mom never took advantage of how people perceived her, however. She would joke about her size and claim that the years of working in the bakery and being able to eat any dessert she wanted took its toll on her figure.

I can remember her swiftly walking through the bakery collecting pans and flour in one hand and cake pans and spoons in the other. She often reminded me of a pack mule when she would walk through the bakery in a hurry to get her next baking project underway. I used to laugh at how quickly she could gather everything and bring it all to the table before most other employees even had a chance to get started. She worked tirelessly, sometimes twelve to fourteen hours a day, never seeming to require rest. I was impressed by her fortitude. I never understood where she got all of her strength.

My grandfather used to say that my mother was as strong as an ox and as stubborn as a mule. I chuckled each time he would say that to my mother. She would look at him with such exasperation on her face, hands on her wide hips, and say, "Come on now Dad. Cut that out."

My grandfather would also tease her relentlessly about her hair. My mother had long brown hair that had grown down below her waist. She kept it pinned up when working at the bakery of course, but that didn't stop my grandfather from teasing her about it.

"You are running so fast through the bakery all of the time that your hair is going to get caught in the mixer," my grandfather would joke.

My mother would usually remark, "You know I don't wear my hair down in the bakery. Stop that."

"One of these days," he said, "somebody's wedding cake is going to end up with a brown moustache on the bride's face made out of your hair. Then what are you going to do?"

Mom would have to laugh at the thought of that image even though she tried hard not to. However, she never denied the speed that he claimed she could move.

I would listen to them for hours as a child. Back and forth the teasing would go until one or both of them got called away to remove a cake from the oven or wait on a customer who had a question about their order. I think my grandfather was grateful for these small reprieves because much to his chagrin, my mother would usually win the teasing match. She hated to lose. The verbal sparring they did just made her stronger. It was that strength that I had come to know and admire so much that soon enough I would only be able to imagine.

I had gone back to the Regime Hospital the week after the daunting visit with my father. I had been told by the hospital when I called the next day that I couldn't see my mother until the following week. I was informed that the hospital was involved in tri-annual training for their employees and that this didn't allow time for escorting visitors. In other words, allowing families to be together wasn't the Regime's top priority, is how I interpreted it.

Although my visit with my father had not gone as expected and left me with such a lost feeling, I wanted to see my mother and receive reassurance that everything was going to be okay. I had done this so many times before when I was growing up. That reassurance had been put on hold until the following week.

Mom always knew just the right thing to say when I was feeling sad about something. One of the earliest memories I have of this happened when I was about six years old. I was an avid animal lover and for as far back as I can remember our family had dogs, cats, rabbits, geese, chickens, and ducks on our property. We weren't rich by any means but because we lived in the mountains, property was more affordable and some of the egg-producing animals actually helped us have food to eat when money was tight.

One of our cats had had kittens. There were five of them in all. The kittens were the cutest creatures that I had ever seen. Constant meowing could be heard most hours of the day and night. It seemed that these kittens were perpetually hungry too. There was a black-and-white one, an orange colored one, a tabby, a blonde colored one, and a calico kitten. I was so happy. I would watch them snuggling up to their mother's belly, a beautiful grey cat, to nurse. Their paws would knead her stomach as they suckled for every ounce of nourishment that she could provide.

As they began to grow, I became more attached to them. Soon they were able to play outside for an extended period of time and they became more adapted to outside living as they grew into early adulthood. One of the young cats, the tabby, appeared a little under the weather one day to my mother, so my mother decided that she needed to take him to the local veterinarian. While we didn't have a crate to carry the cat in, my mother found a cardboard box that appeared to work just fine. She cut plenty of air holes in the box and made a porthole-type window for the cat to see out of as we drove to the vet's office.

The vet's office was about a fifteen-minute drive down a busy two-lane highway. There were no freeways to take to the office at that time because our town was still a small rural town. That wouldn't always be the case, however.

Once the Regime learned about the area and its surrounding mountain vistas, they decided that a freeway would allow more people to enjoy the mountain scenery. That was when my family's home and property had been taken by the government. We were told that we couldn't take anything with us, such as fixtures or the pine paneling that donned the inside walls of our house, adding to the rustic feel of our quaint country home. The Regime owned it now and everything inside. All we had left were our memories.

Once we reached the vet's office my mother parked as close as she could to the building so that a quick shuffling of the box from the car to the office could be achieved without incident. My mother knew that this was the tabby's first ever car ride and first time being carried in a box. She was afraid that it might become frightened and jump out of the box so she wanted to act hastily.

My mother carefully opened the back door of our four-door station wagon and reached in to grab the box. Just at that moment, the tabby seeing its route to freedom, leapt out of the poorly-secured box and into a small wooded area next to the office building. Thankfully, being a small town had its advantages that day. There weren't a lot of cars passing by so the cat was safe for the moment. The tabby quickly disappeared into the woods out of sight, however. We called out its name for what seemed like hours. Most of the time, I believe, had actually been spent calling out to trees and bushes because we never saw the cat, not even once.

The ride back home was quiet and lengthy. I sat next to my mother, crying and wiping away my tears on my pink sweatshirt sleeve. One of the cats that I had grown to love so much was gone from my life forever.

My mother pulled the car over to the side of the road and hugged me for a while. She kept telling me in a sweet and loving voice that she was sorry. My mother told me that she should have never taken the cat to the vet's office without a proper crate. I knew though that my mother had done the best that she could even though I was emotionally hurting from my loss. Even at six years old, I knew that my family could not have purchased a crate because that money was needed for bills and to feed and clothe three children.

Through my hurt, I saw my mother's disappointment in herself that she had let her daughter down by the loss. I could also see that she knew she had endangered the life of the tabby cat. I knew that hurt my mother tremendously because she was just as much of an animal lover as I. She struggled to find the right words to say to me. She comforted me the best way she could. She promised me that everything would work out. She was usually right, but I didn't believe her this time.

A week had passed following our trip to the vet's office with our tabby cat. I had named the cat "Tabby" when he was just a kitten. Not the most inventive of names, but then again I was only six. I felt that it was a great name and described who he was precisely. Now, I could only sit around and wonder what had happened to him.

My mother would come and sit next to me and talk to me about how I was feeling. I would cry a little about how much I missed Tabby and my mother would scoot closer to my side, giving me a gentle hug and a kiss on the head. She would remind me that things would be okay.

As I sat on the porch of our house with my mother listening to her words of encouragement, I looked up for a moment to watch the remaining four cats playing in the yard. They had really grown and were so mischievous now. I thought about Tabby and how he would never get to grow up. I imagined that he had been eaten by some animal or had starved to death. I had seen Disney movies in which similar things happened to unsuspecting poor animals. Bambi was a perfect example because the poor baby deer had lost her parents when they were killed by hunters. I didn't want to think that Tabby had met a similar fate but my childish imagination ran rampant.

Just then, I saw a cat coming toward me from the road. I adjusted my eyes so that I could focus better. I looked again and then tapped on my mother's knee interrupting her conversation. My mother was about to ask me what I wanted when her eye caught a glimpse of what I was seeing.

There right in front of us strolling into the yard was Tabby. It was the same cat! He began meowing and acted as though he had only been gone for a few moments. He walked over to us and started circling my leg, meowing louder each time he repeated the circle, rubbing the top of his head against my ankle. I was staring at him in disbelief.

My mother was the first one to jump up and run to get him something to eat. I didn't want to move because I wanted to stay with him. I didn't want to lose him again. I just kept asking myself if I was looking at a real cat or if I was dreaming. My mother assured me that I wasn't imagining things. She told me that it was truly a miracle that Tabby had somehow made it those ten miles back to us. It was one of the happiest days of my life. My mother had been correct. Everything did turn out all right.

CHAPTER 13:
MOTHER'S DAY

I was hoping that everything would turn out fine the day I sat waiting to see my mother in the Regime Hospital's waiting room. The visitor's room was the same one I had waited in on the day I had visited my father. It had also been a year since I last saw my mother.

As I waited, I recalled that the most recent memory I had at that point of my mother was on the day I saw the Regime vehicle parked on the street in front of our house. I had been walking home after school with my friends from the bus stop one late September afternoon. When I noticed the vehicle, I forgot all about my friends and raced off to the front door to find out why the Regime was there.

Just as I had reached my hand forward to turn the doorknob, two men came rushing out with my parents. I noticed that both of my parents were handcuffed as they passed by me on their way down to the government vehicle waiting at the curb.

I cried out, "Mommy what's happening? Where are you taking my mother?"

"Go inside the house young lady. Your parents are going for a visit. They will be back," one of the Regime men assured me.

The tone of his voice had given me little comfort.

"Bethany, go inside the house," my mother cried out, "We'll be back as soon as we can."

I remember watching as my parents were placed inside the vehicle and driven off hurriedly up the street.

I sat on the front stairs crying for what seemed like hours that day. No one was there to ease my pain.

I was going to have to take care of my sisters and myself, I thought. I would later learn that a couple had "volunteered" to care for us. In actuality, our care had been prearranged by the Regime prior to taking my parents away.

I remember having trouble sleeping that night. I lay in my bed tossing and turning most of the night before eventually giving in to sleep. When I did finally fall asleep it was restless and I had a horrible nightmare.

> *In my dream, I was in an office building with other people that I didn't recognize. I was helping one of the office workers, a woman in her thirties, clean out one of the desks so that I could use it as a place to sit and do my work.*

> *I was cleaning out a drawer and came upon a purse. I considered it odd that someone would leave behind a purse. I thought to myself, she must have been in a hurry. I showed the purse to the woman who had been helping me clear out the desk.*

> *She grabbed the purse from me and starting looking through it. She spotted a wallet inside of it and opened the wallet without hesitation. Instantly, she began to slowly and painstakingly pull a dollar bill out of the wallet.*

> *I was struck by the distinctiveness of this event. She wasn't simply removing a bill from a wallet to perhaps steal the money or to confirm that there was money in the person's wallet. Instead, this act was purposefully orchestrated to direct my full intention at the bill itself.*

> *As I began to stare closely at the face on the dollar bill, I noticed that the face was no longer that of America's first president, George Washington. The face had been replaced by a bust of the leader of the Regime, Mr. Aplitacon himself.*

Almost immediately, I was struck with a foreboding. I felt that my dream was trying to show me that the Regime had completely taken over everything in my country, right down to the monetary system.

I began to frantically call out to God in my dream for protection while trying to hold on to the sense of freedom that I had once known. I awoke with a jolt and a clearer understanding that my dream wasn't far from the reality that I had been facing and that it represented the future of my country.

While sitting in the hospital waiting room, I had become lost in my thoughts about my nightmare. I looked up just in time to see a hospital staff member coming toward me down the hallway. The last time I came here to visit my father I had not been sure of the routine. This time I knew what to expect. The nurse introduced herself and indicated that my mother was on the third floor, room 319.

I had been anxious to see her. I wanted to talk to her again. I wanted her to tell me that everything was going to be okay and that she was okay. I wanted to hear her voice again and see her smile at me. I wanted to hug her and sit next to her. I couldn't wait to tell her what I had been doing and how things were going for my sisters and me. I just wanted to know when she would be coming home. I would find out the answer soon.

The elevator had seemed slower than when I had visited my father. I thought maybe it was because it was earlier in the day or because visitors had not been allowed to come the previous week due to staff training sessions. I waited as the elevator descended from the eleventh floor, then the tenth floor, stopping at the ninth floor presumably to unload and load passengers. I was in the lobby and felt that my chance to get into the elevator wouldn't occur for another lifetime.

Finally, the elevator stopped at the lobby. I moved forward when the doors opened only to have to step back due to the unloading of passengers. An older woman with what looked to be her daughter and her grandchildren made their way off the elevator while talking about what they wanted for lunch. The kids appeared anxious to leave the building. Most likely, having to sit quietly for some time had slowly worn their patience thin.

The family had reminded me of my family back in the days when we were together. My sisters and I had also focused most of our attention on our own needs as children. It didn't occur to me then that the time with my family would be so short. I thought to myself, as I stood there waiting for my turn to enter the elevator, that I wish I could reclaim that time.

The nurse who had been escorting me stepped into the elevator before I saw her do so. I stepped inside right before the elevator doors began to close, a little rattled by almost missing the ride up to my mother's floor. The nurse, realizing that I was nervous, looked up at me, smiled, and then commented on how crowded the elevators seemed that day.

"We're so busy today because we had training last week. Seems like all of the patients' relatives are coming today to make up for lost time," she said.

I smiled a half-baked smile at her but didn't otherwise respond. I was too busy thinking about being reunited with my mother and I didn't want to engage in small talk.

The elevator reached my mother's floor quickly and I was taken to room 319. The nurse stepped inside and walked to the back of the room toward the window. The room was similar to my father's room. It had the same bed, the same nightstand with matching lamp, and the same overstuffed chair. The window was also relatively the same. It allowed in some light but not enough so that you could see out of the window to the outside.

My mother had been sleeping when we walked in. I thought that odd. It was close to eleven in the morning and my mother had always gotten up early. In fact, I'm not sure that my mother ever slept. She would go to bed around eleven o'clock at night and get up at three in the morning, work a full day and then repeat it all over again. I couldn't imagine how she made it through the day. I could only surmise that she was sleepwalking most days.

The nurse had looked at my puzzled expression.

I asked, "Is she asleep?"

The nurse replied, "Yes. She's sleeping more now since she got sick."

I was taken aback for a split second. What do you mean she got sick, I thought to myself? What is she talking about?

I looked at my mother lying on the bed and then my eyes locked onto the nurse's eyes.

"I don't understand, sick with what?"

"Oh, I'm sorry. I thought you had been told. We try to tell the family members but sometimes things fall through the cracks. Everyone gets pretty busy. Don't worry though. We've been taking good care of her."

I had felt my blood pressure beginning to rise. I had wanted to scream at the nurse. I wanted to yell and tell her that if the Regime hadn't taken her from me that I would be the one taking care of her. I would have known what was wrong with her. She was my mother, not the Regime's.

Instead, I turned away from the nurse and looked down at my mother. I was beginning to feel more in control of my emotions and made sure that my voice was at a whisper before I spoke again so as not to disturb my mother's sleep.

"What's wrong with her," I asked.

She suddenly looked like she was at a loss for words. I repeated myself slowly still at a whisper.

"What's wrong with my mother?"

"I'm sorry to have to be the one to tell you but your mother is dying of cancer."

I turned away from my mother and looked directly at the nurse. I couldn't quit staring into her eyes. I kept hoping that the words that had come from her would somehow change if I kept my focus on her. She became uncomfortable and then asked me if I was okay.

She said, "You need to sit down. You're not looking so well."

That had been an understatement. I had felt myself becoming angrier by the second. I kept thinking, how could they? How could they take my mother away from me? How could they not tell me that she was dying? How could they take my mother away from me again? I wanted to yell obscenities. I began to feel that my tears were close to the surface. I didn't want to cry in front of this woman. I didn't need her "help" any longer. No one had taken the time to tell a daughter that the mother she loved was dying. But that was government efficiency, right, I thought to myself? Right!

My mother had begun to move about in the bed. She was moving restlessly, trying to wake up out of her sleep. She opened her eyes and looked straight up at me. I felt that I couldn't hold back my tears any longer. My mother grabbed me with all of the strength that her ailing body could muster and pulled me into her. We hugged and cried for several minutes.

"Bethany, is that you?" my mother asked through tears with a coarseness to her faint voice.

"Mama, it's me. I've missed you so much. What have they done to you?"

I hadn't meant for those last words to come out but it was too late. My mother immediately picked up on my tone of voice.

"No one has done anything, Bethany. It's just that I got sick. Everything is going to be okay."

My mother had once again been trying to assure me that things would be fine, as she had done so many times throughout my childhood. However, this time I knew that my mother didn't believe what she was saying. This time, she was saying it to give me the only thing she had left. She was trying to help me find solace in the situation by her reassurance.

I wouldn't have my mother in my life much longer after that day. I returned to see her on several occasions but on one of my last visits there I knew that it would be the last time that I saw her alive. I stood silently in her room watching her sleep. She slept more those last days and existed more on morphine drips than anything else. I had watched my mother waste away in front of my eyes and there was nothing I could do to stop it. Just like there had been nothing I could do to stop the Regime from taking her out of my life that late September afternoon.

The once robust woman had been reduced to nothing more than skin and bones. So much time had passed. A year was a long time when it turned out to be the last year my mother would spend on this earth, and I had not been able to be a part of it.

As I kissed my mother goodbye, I took one last long look at her. She had drifted off to sleep and the pain had subsided momentarily. I thanked her for being the best mother that any daughter could ever have. I told her I loved her and somewhere deep within her she acknowledged my words and whispered to me in a frail voice that she loved me too.

CHAPTER 14:
THE FINAL GOODBYE

My mother's funeral had been difficult to get through. Our caretakers or "new parents" had brought my sisters and me to the church where my mother had requested to be buried. I had worn a black dress that I had once worn to an evening church function a little over a year before, not knowing then that I would be wearing it for a more ominous occasion in the near future. My sisters had been dressed in black skirts and sweaters with white cotton blouses.

My father had been allowed to attend the funeral as well. He was brought there by the hospital staff. He had been sedated because it was feared that he would start acting out again. My father had been seated next to me. He had been dressed in a black suit that the Regime had donated to him. He sat quietly with his hands folded in his lap.

The church had been modestly decorated with several bouquets of live flowers. Cut flowers were not allowed by the Regime to be used at functions because it was considered destructive to nature. Live flowers could be replanted and enjoyed by the collective after a function or funeral. Also, caskets were no longer used for burial. It had been determined by the Regime—and thus by those that voted them into office—that cremation was a better environmental option because caskets took up too much land.

I didn't know what I felt more saddened about sitting there in the church, the fact that my mother was gone, or the fact that my father, who was still technically living, was also gone. It was almost too much for me to bear. I had never felt more alone in my life than I did at that moment.

Gone were the people that had guided me into adulthood, the people who cared for me without regard to their own desires. They had been great parents who encouraged my sisters and me to grow and be happy. They believed in us and our abilities. They supported us in whatever we wanted to do regardless of how silly our childish plans might have sounded. And, they taught us life's lessons that we would need now that they were gone.

As I sat in the church listening to people at the podium speaking about how my mother had touched their lives, I remembered telling my mother when I was just six years old that I wanted to be an astronaut and a doctor.

> *"Mommy, can I be an astronaut, a doctor, or maybe both when I grow up?" I asked.*

> *"I don't see why not, sweetie," my mother replied as she smiled down at me.*

> *We had been watching television together that morning and a show came on in which several professionals were being interviewed about their careers. Instead of telling me that I probably needed to only choose one profession or the other, or that it was most likely impossible to afford to send me to school for either career on my parents' salaries, my mother looked deeply into my eyes and lovingly said, "You'll make the best astronaut and doctor in the world."*

> *Those words, spoken by my mother, to an overly ambitious six-year-old, convinced me at that very moment that I could do anything because my mother believed that I could.*

I wasn't sure I still believed that sitting there at my mother's funeral that day. I couldn't imagine how I was going to be able to go on without her. No longer would I hear her encouragement. I was stuck; stuck in a world that I no longer recognized sitting next to a man that I no longer knew.

Life had changed drastically since my youth growing up with my parents and sisters. As I sat there, I looked over at my sisters and saw their anxiousness to leave. They weren't as much missing our mother as they were anxious to return to the home and the culture they now fully embraced with our "new parents" and "new lives." They were at our mother's funeral mainly out of obligation, or at least that's how it seemed to me.

I had yearned for another day, just one more day to see my mother so happy in her bakery working next to my grandmother, talking about a wedding cake that had to be baked and decorated for an upcoming large wedding to be held at the Catholic Church. I wanted one more day to hear my mother and grandfather teasing each other about my mother's hair, or to see her and my father sitting at our kitchen table discussing their plans for us for Easter.

I knew I would no longer have those moments. Those moments that I had believed would be there forever had been reduced to memories that I would desperately need to carry in my heart.

CHAPTER 15:
WHAT MATTERS MOST

I was beginning to think that my life had become just a series of memories about how life used to be before the Regime robbed me of my family and a major part of my life, namely my childhood and early adulthood. I have spent hours reflecting on the past. For over twenty-one years following my mother's death my focus has seemingly been on nothing else accept my past. I've been lost in my own thoughts about the way things used to be, so much so that I'm afraid I've stopped living in the present.

This wasn't the way I had intended to live my life nor was it what my parents had hoped my life would be. As a child, I was like any other typical kid growing up in a loving family. A family that worked hard, provided for their own family, and helped others out as often as they were financially able. They instilled these same values in me along with a sense that there were great things to come in my life if I was willing to put forth the effort to reach my goals.

My parents had also taught me that I lived in the greatest country in the world. America, they said, was a place where immigrants dreamed of coming to fulfill their dreams and to be free. It was a country, they promised, that welcomed all people for a better life.

That had all changed once the Regime came into power. It seems that the Regime had convinced the majority in this country that they, not the people, knew what was best for them. Individual freedom was no longer valued. The collective was all that mattered.

Men and women in America had been willing to listen because they were trying to manage so many things at once. Between working, attending school, raising kids, buying homes, and taking care of aging parents, having someone promise to unburden the load was a welcome relief. The people of America began to do more than just listen. They bought into the philosophy of the Regime. They began to follow along rather than pay attention to what they were losing in the process.

At first, the Regime made simple changes that didn't cause great alarm to the average person. The Regime quickly established a partnership with parents by focusing on the needs of children. Parents were in favor of this philosophy.

Parents were sold on the Regime's philosophy by being told that they wanted to help moms by giving school-aged children a healthy meal to eat. Parents, moms especially, were soon convinced that they weren't providing appropriately nutritious meals for their own children. The shift in thinking began in a non-blaming approach by the distribution of nutritional information to assist loving parents who were just misguided. It evolved into a condemnation of parenting when parents didn't want to change their "archaic" ways fast enough for the Regime.

Parents were assured by the Regime that extensive research had been conducted into what was considered proper parenting for raising healthy children. The Regime told parents that they were merely there to partner with them and to assist in raising their awareness. How could anything be wrong with that? Doesn't everyone want children to grow up healthy and well adjusted?

After a while, the parents just stopped arguing and agreed that as a parent, they didn't have enough knowledge in the matter without the Regime's help.

Once the Regime had mastered the parenting market, they began to set their focus on the public in general. First, the public was told that they needed to eat better, choose smaller portions, and consume more balanced meals. Again, people listened and once again people believed. Before they knew it, the Regime was making appropriate food selections mandatory for the collective. Any restaurant in violation of allowing a customer to purchase what the Regime deemed unhealthy would be fined and ultimately driven out of business. The media also helped to promote the Regime's agenda.

Many businesses didn't realize until it was too late that they would be held accountable for their customer's choices. It was a rude awakening for those owners who felt that it would make things easier on them to allow the Regime to set the standards. They wouldn't need to decide what was healthy and what wasn't because the Regime had made a list of items that they deemed unhealthy. Everything else was okay to sell. However, it became obvious once the list was published that most of the items on the list were highly-sought after items by the general public.

For example, no longer would salt be allowed to be purchased. Too much salt raised the blood pressure of those people not in top shape, according to the Regime's esteemed scholars. Butter was also eliminated. It was felt that butter contained too much fat to be considered healthy. Thus, the need for milk-producing cows was also reduced because they were no longer needed to produce butter.

The cows could have been used as meat but meat, the Regime stressed, was one of the most harmful items that a person could consume. The meat was proven to clog arteries and led to early heart attacks in some people. If the people weren't willing to acknowledge these damaging facts on their own then the Regime would have to step in and protect them from themselves. More fruits and vegetables were promoted to maintain a healthy balance.

At first it was comical to watch this philosophy being thrust upon the American people. Most initially saw this as something that would sooner or later fail because it was thought that no one would ever believe or accept this line of reasoning. America had been a country that prided itself on individual freedom. Surely, no one would stand by and allow the government to tell them what they could or couldn't eat. They were wrong.

The Regime was eventually seen as being the authority on nutrition. It was just a matter of time before the majority of people began to concede that the Regime possessed this supreme knowledge. People began to believe that the Regime was acting in their best interest because the government had swayed most people to believe that they could no longer choose wisely for themselves.

Next, our religious freedoms came under attack. The majority of the citizens in America were Christian at the time. Our country had been founded on Christian principles. The Regime, however, started to express concern that that the Christian way of thinking had become outdated. Christian values were all about the family, a mother, father, and children living together with the parents having been married after taking the vows espoused in their Christian Bible.

Most families today, according to the Regime, were made up of couples of the opposite sex, same sex, or single parents living together under one roof. They believed that this was the more accurate and modern definition of family.

It was believed by the Regime that those families that didn't meet the definition of the traditional Christian family would feel judged. If they felt judged then this could potentially make them feel unequal to everyone else. That possibility was not acceptable to the Regime. Everyone must be and feel equal in every aspect of their lives to everyone else according to the government's viewpoint.

This belief system prompted the Regime to establish laws that attacked the very tenets of Christianity. At first, Christians fought hard to keep their beliefs intact. In the end, however, after the media had portrayed them as villains and destroyed their once favorable public persona, many Christians surrendered the fight. They came to agree that the Regime's newer attitude of making people feel more comfortable might be more equitable than upholding the ancient tenets of a religion.

That was when I knew that I could no longer be a part of what my country had become. It was the breaking point for me. I had tolerated as much as I could for as long as I could. However, once the principles of Christianity were lost, I knew I had to disengage from the country that the Regime had developed around me.

It was difficult at first. I felt terribly alone. I had lost both of my parents and I never was able to find out where my grandparents had been taken once they had been moved from the Regime's hospital. I presumed that they had not been able to survive the Regime's "retraining" process.

I had also become distant from my sisters, as well. They felt that I was unreasonable in regards to my beliefs and that I should just "get with the program." They believed that their lives had improved since the Regime took over. In their many discussions with me, trying to convince me to abandon the "error of my ways," they had stated their frustrations with my failure to accept the benefits of living under the Regime. To them, there were no negatives in following the Regime's guidelines. In fact, one of my sisters felt that the Regime's newer views of a broader spirituality was closer to her own beliefs, even though she had been raised in a Christian household by our parents.

I had no one to turn to and no place to go where I felt I fit in. I thought it was ironic that in the Regime's perfect world of "equality" that I didn't feel equal to anyone else. Just the opposite was true. I felt that unless I gave up my common sense and personal freedoms that I would never be accepted or seen as an equal to anyone who now adhered to the Regime's way of thinking.

I didn't give up hope, however. I knew there had to be other people out there who felt just like I did. Most of my friends and relatives had given up a long time ago and started to follow the Regime's rules without question. I didn't know how to find the people who were like me; those that had not surrendered. However, I knew that I wanted to connect with them, if for nothing else then to have an intelligent conversation with someone who remembered what it was like when we could make our own choices and think for ourselves. A time when it was okay to choose and be wrong if that was what was needed in order to learn and grow. I knew that growth was not possible when someone else controlled your every decision.

I decided that I would sooner live on my own as a homeless person rather than continue living in the hell that the Regime had created. If you were homeless you weren't seen as an equal. However, it was the only choice that the Regime allowed its' citizens to make for themselves. It was thought that if you were not smart enough to grasp the benefits of living life the Regime way, then you were of no further value to the Regime or the collective. You could live on the streets at the mercy of others, if there was any to be found, until you regained your senses and came back to the Regime. If not, you could live on the streets until you died.

I never regained "my senses" by agreeing to accept the Regime's control over me. I can't say that life has been easy being homeless, but when I reflect back I realize that I probably started down the path of becoming homeless the day the Regime forcefully removed my parents from our home.

I did eventually begin to discover others who shared in my beliefs. It took me years before I felt confident enough to cautiously engage others in conversation to determine if they were genuinely on the side of the Regime or not. I got to know others who had also decided that they could no longer sit idly by and wait while their very souls were taken from them.

We would gather in creek beds and in parks during the day when most people were watching television. There we would discuss how things used to be. At times, we would ponder the questions of how everything had happened so quickly and why no one had tried to stop it. Ultimately, we knew we already held the answers to the questions. We knew how the Regime had wormed its way into the minds of people before they even understood what was happening.

Our purpose in the beginning had been to merely console each other. We were shoulders to cry on for each other and ears to listen to the many woes of those who had lost so much. Sadly, some in our group had committed suicide in order to escape what they had described as "inescapable pain." While I saw many desperate people and also felt defeated at times, I knew that suicide was not the path for me. My parents had taught me to fight. My parents had fought up to the very end and there was no way that I could disgrace their memory by taking the easy way out.

So many suicides began to change the purpose and direction I had originally thought I had taken. I stopped dwelling on the past or how bad things had gotten under the Regime leadership and began focusing on ideas and strategies for turning things back around to the way they used to be. I was determined to find a way to regain the freedoms I once knew. I didn't want to continue losing hope or seeing others self-destruct because they saw no better way out.

I came to understand that there was only one way to really survive the life in which we now found ourselves following the election and installation of the Regime. We needed to continue our separate lives, but in so doing we needed to work together to create a system within a system.

At first, the thoughts of this didn't make sense even to me and it was my idea. How was this to be accomplished? Could it be accomplished? These thoughts would soon develop into conversations with other people whom I had come to trust.

Some of our first strategy meetings took place in an abandoned office building that no longer produced the items that were once considered popular. One of our conversations, in fact, had taken place in the same bakery that my mother and grandmother used to work. Now the sights and sounds of the once bustling and happy bakery had been replaced by cobwebs, dust, and dirt. The electricity had been turned off years before and the ovens and mixing machines sat covered in heavy dust after many years of neglect.

Sitting on an old wooden crate that used to carry gallons of milk from one station to the other so that cakes, pies, and cookie dough could be made, I couldn't help but be reminded of how many people had lost their jobs and given up their dreams since the Regime had made the determination that this business was no longer viable because it produced what the Regime considered harmful to the public.

My mother and grandmother had not put their blood, sweat, and tears into the bakery so that the government could rip it away from them. My mother had hoped to buy the business from the owner. It only made sense because she ran the business and was more involved in running it than the owner chose to be. She had dreamed of leaving the business to her family. She had hoped that my sisters and I would be working side-by-side, carrying on the tradition of hard work, creativity, and pride in a craft. Those dreams, once a possibility, were now gone forever.

Now, the bakery was a gathering place of minds dedicated to rebuilding a once great country. There were seven of us at this particular meeting, including a husband and wife I had met a couple of years ago after the wife had miscarried their first child. I had learned that it had been an unexpected pregnancy but they were looking forward to having the baby. After the miscarriage, both of them felt that they couldn't handle the world around them anymore. They were frustrated with struggling to survive mentally and physically in a country they no longer recognized. Three older adult men in their forties and a younger woman in her early thirties had met each other and then joined our small group as we began to build a rapport with them.

We were eager to plan the rebuilding of our country. It was a daunting task and not one that we were sure we were capable of completing. However, we realized that if we didn't attempt to do so all hope would be lost in trying to regain some semblance of what we used to know.

As we sat around on old boxes and disintegrating bakery tables, I posed the first question.

"Could there be an existence or system that would be able to function within a larger system? You know, a micro system within a much larger macro system," I said to those gathered at the meeting.

My question was met with what seemed like a long period of silence. Vacant stares appeared on faces that searched for a sign that I had been joking or that they had somehow misunderstood my question.

But I wasn't joking and there had been no misunderstanding. I was serious about my plan. Had it ever been done in the history of America? I didn't know but I was willing to try anything at that point.

It was the woman's husband that was the first to break the long silence.

"I've never thought of something like that, but who's to say it won't work? Does anybody else have a better idea?"

I was thankful for the response. It made me feel that I wasn't as crazy as I had felt a few minutes before when I asked the question.

"We'll need to continue trying to reach out to find others to join us," I continued. "Slowly 'retraining' people on the ideas that once worked so well in our country must be our goal."

One of the men in his forties tried to interrupt but I kept talking.

"I'm certain that it won't be easy. However, we have to start someplace," I said.

"But, it's going to be dangerous," the man in his forties continued this time.

"I know," I said. "In the beginning, we are going to have to work surreptitiously so the Regime won't figure out what we are trying to accomplish."

I wasn't too worried at this point, however, about being admonished or arrested by the Regime if we were suspected of speaking out against them as long as we remained a small group. They had become so confident in their ability to convince others in "Aplitacon" that their philosophy was the only key to success. So much so, that they didn't suspect that anyone would try to overthrow their leadership. I believed that their overly-confident egos would eventually lead to their demise as long as we were careful in selecting the right people with whom to associate.

"We need to start building communities of individuals made up of families that will begin to grow and provide their own food for themselves and each other," I said. "We will have to figure out how we can supply our own electricity, medical needs, and housing."

After a slight pause, I continued on. "We must find the people who have the brain power to recreate what has been taken from us. We are literally going to have to start over and we must do everything right under the noses of the Regime without being recognized as a real threat."

I asked myself silently once the words were out, could we really do it? It was yet to be seen.

"Just like our forefathers did in the founding of America, we must find that same spirit that made the country what it once was: strong, innovative, and free," I continued. "The best minds are out there and we need to win back their support. You know who they are," I said with emphasis.

"They are those people that once had been able to grow their medical practices, small businesses, and corporations with the intent of achieving their own American dream. We will have to seek out those people that have given up on thinking that they would ever see a resurgence of capitalism and personal achievement in their lifetime," I said with conviction.

The couple was the first to stand up and proclaim their commitment to the plan I had set forth. Ours was a plan to take back our country and return it to its rightful owner.

Those in attendance that day, the seven self-appointed revolutionaries, would commit to fighting for the return of the freedom that had once been possessed by all. It wouldn't be an easy task, but it would be a path developed by one person—one individual at a time.

We would have our memories to rely on to get it right this time. We knew on that day that we might never live long enough to see the fruits of our labor. However, we felt confident that our efforts would someday result in a generation that would carry the torch and continue the fight for freedom, the freedom that their parents, grandparents, and great-grandparents had once been given by their Creator.

"God bless America," we exclaimed together as we took the first steps in reclaiming our right to the country we had once been given by God Himself.

ABOUT THE AUTHOR

SUSAN CALLOWAY KNOWLES is a Licensed Christian Marriage and Family Therapist, former Family Law Attorney, and an aspiring Christian Songwriter.

Susan is a contributor to several Christian websites writing articles of inspiration for those interested in developing a closer relationship with the Holy Spirit. Her articles can be found at www.crosswalk.com , www.believe.com , and www.womenwhothrive.com.

Her song, "Follow Me" is a tribute to her love for God and can be found at www.worshipsong.com or on her personal website at www.susanknowles.com.